Born in the Iraqi city of Basra, Nofel Nawras grew up in Brighton
and Southend before moving to London where he trained as
an actor at the Guildhall School of Music and Drama. He later
studied creative writing at Falmouth University, where he
was awarded a first-class degree. His poetry and short stories
have been published in literary publications including *Conscious
Shift*, *Zeitgeist Spam* and *Adelaide Literary Magazine*. *Brighton
Funk* is his first book. Nofel lives in Cornwall.

Brighton Funk

Nofel Nawras

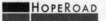

HopeRoad Publishing
PO Box 55544
Exhibition Road
London SW7 2DB

www.hoperoadpublishing.com
@hoperoadpublish

First published in Great Britain by HopeRoad 2022
Copyright © 2022 Nofel Nawras

A CIP catalogue record for this book is available from the British Library.

ISBN: 978-1-913109-86-8
eISBN: 978-1-913109-92-9

For Molly

One

The old man's insane. Hates like a lunatic and looks like one
as well. Nothing inside but black stuff. Black tar, bile and
vomit. He looks at me, spits in my face, and I stand there. I
know what's coming, I know what happens by now. I hold my
breath and wait. All this appears on the outside. It's what we
see, understand, and mostly we're okay with it, even if it's
mad. Then there's the collapse, the reveal. Something happens
that's never happened before. It breaks through the surface
grime that covers things up. This is one of those moments. I
do something. Nothing amazing. Barely noticeable.

Courage comes when you least expect it. Comes out of
nowhere, leaves a singing in your chest, a sunshine inside,
a lightness. When it's over, it's done, complete. You might
smile. You might not. It's not arrogance. I don't know what it
is. There must be something inside that's connected to God.
Not the church tosh. Not that religious crap. Something
you can't name. The weird thing is it's always the same but
always new. A door opens. Some parallel dimension we've
forgotten. It sucks you home. You're a star in your own film.

There's this thing called *out of body experience*. It sometimes happens when people are dying or in shock. They see everything from another place, out of their body. With courage you're in your body. You don't leave it. It takes over, and you vanish. There's no fear. A power snaps in, and you're doing what you can only dream about. No umming and aahing, no *Oh dear, what shall I do?* It's too fast. You're in there, and it's poetry, beautiful. You might be taking on more than you can chew, but it doesn't matter. Matter's gone out the window. You're in, and when you're done, you're out. No more, no less.

Talking of vanishing, me and Johnny went to see *Vanishing Point* last Sunday afternoon. They let anyone in the Odeon. It smells of manky dogs and stale piss. Such a tip. Needs decimating, exterminating, vanishing. Most days it's empty apart from dirty old men who come and sit behind you. They start pushing your seat from behind with their knees. One day I had enough. I got up and told the nonce to lay off in no uncertain terms. Caused a right old stir. Manager came down and chucked me out. No refund. The perv was smiling as I left.

Vanishing Point was fantastic. Fast cars, drugs and beautiful women. Something else. It was well mystical, man. A journey into our times. Cosmic. Beyond the hippy cool and happenings there was something else. I love those films that make you wonder about stuff, they seem to hit a place that lights up inside. The hero wasn't way out. Just a geezer caught up in the madness. He pushed it. Pushed the boundaries, the surface of things. Vanished.

Back to the old man. He's doing his freak-out routine with his blood vessels about to explode, eye whites crimson, and I'm still standing there, waiting. It's his *Danse Macabre* (listened to that in English last week), a wave of frustrated hate sounds exploding all over each other, cutting deep into the air ... picture a clown up to his neck in horse muck, drowning in it ... spittle flying with expletives, machine-gun bullets, jagged glass cutting through baby-soft flesh.

Usually when people chunter, there're about four things going on. There's the *Sussing of the situation*. There's the *Do I want to be here?* There's the *What can I get out of this?* And there's the *How do I go about getting it?* The other planks are doing the same so there's as much chance of any real communication as winning the pools. Thing is, someone does every now and then, and when they do, I reckon they might have a glimpse of that other place. Seems daft we can only get there in extreme situations.

I hold his gaze. Whoa. What the hell am I doing? I'm here, now. Nothing inside. No me, no him. I see into him, and he sees I'm seeing. Contact. Communication. Silent. The outer noise goes on, the movement. It's a million miles away. Me and him, here, in the centre. We both know. Words are redundant. They can't compete. This, whatever it is, says everything.

He sees ... it sends ripples through his animal brain, and in that fraction of a second his eyes look with a different glint. Confusion, reassessment, readjustment. That's when I do what I do. Some other part of who I am rises, and I clench my right fist. Hardly noticeable. An animal reaction. No. It's more than that. It's everything I am. All the years of my life. The who I am, what I am, who I might become, Christ knows. Not like it's going to *do* anything. A simple clenching of a fist. A fist that says *Go on then, get on with it.We both know what's coming. I don't give a toss.You can hurt me, but you can't really hurt me.*

Well. It didn't come. The usual. What came was worth everything, what came was something that would live with me forever. He realised we'd gone past some point of *no return*. He wouldn't admit it. Not out here where we pretend. So he spewed and fumed, spat, said he saw I was clenching, saw I was defending myself. Tried to shrug it off, laugh it off. Big deal ... but it was. We both knew something had happened. A line had been crossed.

Two

'You know what he's like, just do what he says and keep out of his way.' Mum's in one of her moods because the old man's in one of his. His whole life is a mood of varying degrees. Somewhere, I feel sorry for the poor git, but not for long. I remember who he is and tighten up inside. Hate has a tender feeling of familiarity that keeps you balanced. It's a mate in times of lightness and dark.

'But he's wrong, mum.' I'm behind the café counter making teas for some customers, and she's sat in the chair by the window reading *Woman's Realm*. She's got that irritated look on her face that doesn't want to talk about what she knows is mental.

'For Pete's sake, Naseem, when has he ever been right?'

'Can you hear what you're saying?' It makes me boil because I know mum knows he's mad, I know he's mad, Theba, our dog, knows he's mad. In fact, most people in Brighton are in on it, but no one does anything about it. Why? Why do we not confront the insane? Fear. 'Why d'you put up with it? I don't have any choice until I leave … but what about you?'

'Shut up and make the tea. I do not want to talk about this. He can see you, and he knows we're talking about him. Now please, I don't want any more agro,' she said and left, taking her fags, heading upstairs. I can't win. There's a horrible taste in my mouth from upsetting her, but sometimes I have to speak. It doesn't help. She's pained by everything, knows what I'm saying is right but has to live with it. I can't wait to leave this madhouse.

The old man's outside with his brush and paint. He's quite an artist when he wants to be, when he has to be. One of the four large glass panels of our café/house is getting a makeover. Never one to spend money on professionals, out of necessity he turns his hand to anything. His face is always dark, but with the sun behind him it's even worse, and although it's boiling, he's wearing his Mongolian black-and-white knitted hat, thick black jumper, rolled at the sleeves. There's a fag sticking out of the left side of his mouth at an angle of forty-five degrees, and his eyes are squinting as he paints. I can tell his mood by his face, and it's not jolly.

There's a hate that builds up over the years that sediments, turns to poison. It lives down in the depths of your innards and waits. When you're little it has no power, no place to take root. There's too much lightness in your body that helps destroy any dark and moves you on. If the dark keeps building you start to know a constant fear that shadows everything. All you want is a miracle. Someone to play with, have fun with, laugh and take time to be with you. Inside your fresh system you have to make sense of the day to day. There's no one to turn to in a nuclear family. Everyone's drowning in the same stagnant pond.

6

Years go by, and you live the lie until you hardly notice the difference unless you stray out of your prison. You go from one mental institution to another, and as they're all run on the same basis, it's cushty. Once in a while, a sliver of light pierces the fog when you see something different. A pulse comes up from inside that's so intimate, a familiar smell of ancient flowers. It might be a smile on someone's face, a child playing in a park. Best to push those monkeys away and get back to the hate. The hate you can handle.

My dad's a Cossack, a warrior, at least that's what he likes to think. A cross between Yul Brynner and Omar Sharif. If you've ever seen that film with Brynner where he's a Cossack chief, Taras Bulba, that's my dad, only dad's worse. No one knows what other families are like, you might have an idea, but you never know; we've all got secrets. You never really know anyone, not even yourself. Grimy little secrets. Some you get to find out, others it's best not to.

In movies, books, comics, I run away from *The Big Lie*. It's so big nobody talks about it. It's so big we can't. We wouldn't know where to begin because everyone's doing it. It's how we get along. We're all a bunch of liars. You can't tell anyone. They don't want to know. They're all wrapped up in their own lie, having a whale of a time and don't come around here with your silly nonsense. Only thing to do is join in. If you don't there's probably something wrong with you. Screw loose. They'll send you to a trick-cyclist. *The Big Lie* begins with family when mum and dad row, make up, and everything's okay. Only it isn't.

Growing up is a paperchase leaving a trail of boxes in your brain where you keep those secrets I was talking about. They lead back to one big nothing. Out of that nothing you sprang into some home, some country. It's a fresh box, green and tender. All it needs is some recognition, food, warmth. It depends on your postmark as to where you'll end up. You could land in Alaska or Swindon.

People open your original box and have a right laugh to begin with, and then it starts splitting into twos and threes. The idiots keep putting stuff in your boxes, and they grow like a lizard's tail. Bits fall off and bits grow on top of each other, sometimes you live in one, sometimes another or a mixture. There's a safety switch that covers your back when you need to be insane and live in the world, a sort of angel/ devil that messes with your future and past by laying traps in the present. After a while, it almost seems alright, okay to be insane, as long as you make out you're not. Like I said, most people are doing the same, so it's normal to be in one box and out of another. I suppose that's where the phrase *He's out of his box* comes from.

Three

They're having another row. Mum and Taras. Their bedroom door's shut and Jamal and Iman are sitting halfway up the stairs to the second floor. Their faces are taut, gaunt, and Jamal has tears coming down like a dripping tap. He's not bawling, not making a noise. He's listening intently, knowingly, crapping himself, literally. Iman has her arm around him. It's always around him. It's like a shape she can't undo. It's robotic, automatic. I bet she does it in her sleep when they cuddle together in their manky bed with manky covers and manky blankets.

Jamal sucks his filthy comfort cloth and looks at me for help, something, anything. He's frightened of me as well. I'm the one who does nothing. I'm the one who a few years ago bullied him and his sister. Why? Why do that to a helpless toddler? I'm dark inside and move away from any sense of guilt, any explanation. I am what I am, and that's all there is to it. I'm a victim of the sins of the fathers, my father, and I hate him to the depths of my being. I want everyone to suffer like I suffered, still suffer, under his venom, his bile, his spit

9

that he smears me with psychologically, his spit that sprays my face.

You tell me why I have no love to give to my brother and sister. You take me to a lah-di-dah trick-cyclist and let the tosser dissect my entrails and come up with the wrong answer, the wrong solution and never move from the point of no light, no life, nothing. I am alone, I hate, and nothing will change. I grab some bags of crisps and a couple of cans of Coke from the kitchen that's some sort of limbo shadowland where sadness clings to every atom and no warmth dares enter the grim dark pretending to be form and matter.

Hate is strength and power. Hate is delight and sparkles, twinkles, in the gloaming, and I am able to laugh inside at the insanity of it all. My hate can pass through concrete, through form and matter and somehow reach its target. Not the little ones. I spare them my insane, obsidian dark. I'm too grown up now, too distant from their field of sorrow. They need no help from me. They have enough fear in them and lack of love to blaze a rocket to Mars.

'Come on, you two, let's go and watch TV in my room.' They look at me as if I'm Christ, as if a door has opened into a *Star Trek* portal, turn to each other, trying to make sense of what's happening, gauge which nightmare is worse. They get up holding one other, traipse upstairs, and I follow.

Through the dead, flimsy walls that haven't tasted the smell of paint or wallpaper since Noah and his sons built the Ark, Taras is having a mare. Poor mum, poor, unloved woman who gives everything and gets naff all back apart from grief, beatings, snide comments, cutting remarks and is never good enough, never right, always wrong. The man she chose so long ago, the man she must have fallen in love with once upon a fairy-tale time, the man that is calcified hate, is always right, even though he knows he isn't. I'd like to face him. I'd like to have the courage to stand my ground and take him on. I'd like to hurt him like he hurts everyone.

There're all sorts of monsters in this psychedelic playground. Fear has to be one of the top dogs in the manor. It's a black rain that's acid. It burns the flowers, poisons the streams. All well and good running from it, blagging it, trying to laugh it away. It doesn't wash. One day there's a meet-up down a dark and dingy alleyway that has no escape. I push it away, and it makes me small. It makes me hate myself a bit more. I remember our plank of a headmaster talking about fear in assembly last year. He said the only way to deal with it is to see it for what it really is, a ghost. I'd like him to come and have a gas with the ghost downstairs that's taking its venom out on someone I love.

Anyone with a bit of nous avoids a prat who carries around his misery and tries to share it. Behind closed doors it's not always an option to do a runner. Behind closed doors there's a smell of something that has no name. It's a place where, if there is a God, he must have nipped out for a fag. After a while you can get used to anything. Sort of. It's all you know. You get used to the sounds of beatings, the silence of the beaten. You get used to the madness of any situation. Piece of cake.

I turn the TV on loud, give the little waifs the crisps and cans, close the door and walk away.

Four

It's 1972. I'm fifteen and a half years old, been wagging the dog for three. Nobody tells you anything, no one you can trust. You find out for yourself, and it's usually wrong. Amazing how it happens, well, it was in my case. There's all this jabber at school, everyone calls each other everything under the sun, but no one dares talk about it. Christ, that would be so out of order. Anyway, long story short. The sex talk gets quite frequent after twelve; you hear older lads having a laugh at someone else's expense and follow suit. We're all a bunch of apes. The hormones kick in and you enter a new world. The little kid that played with Action Man has gone. Now you're the action man. The sex mags you've borrowed from your mates get you tingling, excited, but then what? Well, one thing leads to another as they say and ... *Christ! What was that?*

Secrets. You hide them under a sweet smile and a joke. Those head boxes have all sorts of labels. One of those Big Daddies lives down a rat-infested sewer you pretend isn't there. It's morphed into a black chest the size of a small hippo labelled *The Twilight Zone* where you keep things you can't deal with. Only place you can release it is in playground confessionals. Wrap up the juiciest bits of sick in tinsel and chuck it at your mates because no other plank's going to listen. Make a joke and live with the nightmare. Your family's no good, they're up to their necks in their own faecal matter. Teachers? Leave it well out. *Are you trying to bunk off, sonny my lad? Stop being a big girl's blouse. Go on, get out before I cane you.*

There's a nightmare. Some sort of prison to herd unwanted animals. Secondary Modern. About as modern as *Oliver Twist*. He could tell a tale, old Charlie. *A Tale of Two Cities*, my favourite. Yeah, I like reading. It's a bit sad, but no one else knows, except mum, and she reads for England.

I'd like to be a writer. Not a hope in hell but who knows, miracles do happen. Books have always been my mates, not that I haven't got mates, but books are different. They speak another language, know you without knowing you. You can wander down the garden path, the Himalayas, the moon, with an invisible blanket wrapped around you even when it's snowing, pouring, storming it ... you can be somewhere sunny, easy. There's no ugliness except what you know will somehow, eventually, rightly, be overcome. In books, people like one another, love one another, do anything for each other. Then there's the journey, the obstacles, the darkness you have to encounter, go through. Books make sense of everything, and yeah, they may not be real, made up, but I don't see it like that. A good book makes more sense than this mad nightmare of a place. Open a book and it's all there, waiting.

Five

A couple of years ago, life took on a whole new psychedelic flavour: I went to my first disco. Didn't know what a disco was. Looking back, I think I must have had a duff gene. I've probably still got it. It's not like you can lose a gene. Anyway, the disco, it was on a Saturday afternoon in this abandoned church, around the corner from Taras Bulba café. I've lived in cafés and restaurants most of my life. There are some advantages. Chips. Burgers and chips, chicken and chips, fish and chips. Oh, and Coke.

My schoolmates said to come along, but I knew Taras wouldn't let me go. He's a teeny-weeny bit insane. Totally. So I told him, through mum, that I was going to play football. Twelve years old, dressed in my best, which wasn't much, clothes not being high on the family agenda, carrying a rucksack with boots and footy gear. Off to the new world. The disco was run by some geezers I didn't recognise. They looked like Arabs, but they weren't. Persians. Arabs and Persians don't mix. Next-door neighbours that hate each other's daylights. They do look similar in manner and dress.

Colourful tear-drop shirts, wide flares, skin-tight around the crotch. Curly, bouffant hair styled to an inch. Medallions, gold bracelets and stinking of Aramis. Look like they'd kill people and painfully tried to smile as they took your money, stamped something inky on the back of your hand. The first initiation.

There were these manky refreshments on a wonky table, crisps, pop, chocolate bars. That was it. It was heaving with at least seventy kids in a dusty church with little alcoves, spooky corridors and a dancefloor. The lights were psychedelic, the music loud, the kids were excited and ... there were girls.

Girls are off limits. One of the many unwritten laws of Taras. Christ knows why. I've been surrounded by mini-skirts, snogging punters, jukeboxes wailing about love and broken hearts. There was always sex jabber in a roundabout way, and when the hormones kicked in I realised I was no different. So what's all this *love* tosh? As far as I could make out it was a one-way street, soppy stuff girls go through, dreaming romantically in an airy-fairy way. Blokes just want sex. I've never met one that's happy with the same bint for long.

Then it happened. I was on the way home from school when something weird came over me. I stopped chuntering in my bonce, and without knowing why I turned around, looked back down the street. An ordinary day, people, traffic, sunshine. There she was. There was a light all around her. She wasn't astonishingly, amazingly, way-out spectacularly beautiful. In fact, she might have been quite ordinary to most people. Short blonde hair, almost white, white skin. She walked, she actually walked like a normal human being and was going somewhere. Daft. Why would you go anywhere? Why would you need to? What am I talking about? I don't know. It's all stopped, vanished. It's all gone grey. No. It is grey ... always been grey, and she ... is *colour*. She is life. Everything else is dead. What everything else? There's nothing else. Nothing.

It's not as if I hadn't seen other attractive girls, but I'd never felt anything other than the usual excitement. This was something else which left me a bit mystified. Maybe I was going to die because my whole body ... froze. Sometimes at the flicks there's a bit where the film goes into slow motion. This was it, and I knew without knowing (I know that sounds daft) what it was. It was love. It wasn't infatuation, it wasn't sex, all the stuff I didn't have a clue about. There was no wanting about it. Sounds crazy, sounds a bit mental, but there was a big hole in my chest, and this mixture of light and angels' singing poured out. Poetic. That's Mr Easton's fault, our English teacher, the only one in our dump of a school that gives a toss. I'd never thought English would be so much fun as it's always struck me as being something brainy, dry, but not with *Easy Easton*. His lessons are the only time I learn anything. It's not shoved down your throat till you're sick or empty drivel you couldn't care less about, stuff that puts you to sleep. It's real, about people, about life and death, it makes you wonder.

Would Mr Easton say it was love? Yeah, I think he would; maybe he'd remember something in his own experience. The thing is, he's honest in a way not many are around here. Everyone's in their own private nightmare, trying to make ends meet, having rows, babies, eating and lying. Being honest is not on the menu. People scream *Tell the truth!* if they think you've nicked a few bob, but being honest isn't about that. It's something else. Short-story short ... I was in love. Hold up, kids can't fall in love, that's general knowledge, common sense. As if love is common.

Six

The disco ... awesome, mind-blowing. One of the first songs I danced to was 'Black Night' by Deep Purple. I can't stand heavy metal, it does my nut, never usually touch it with a bargepole, but everyone was doing their thing and I needed to find mine. I'd never tasted this level of wildness. The buzz was eating up my head space, chucking out the fear, the shakes. All I had to do was jump into a sea of arms, legs, bodies that pulsed, jerked and no one cared who you were, where you came from. I was in head first. You didn't have to jabber, worry about what to say. The odd thing about the song was how it seemed to be saying the same thing. It hammered out sound bombs, flame-throwing words about not giving a toss, not being afraid. Christ, maybe I'm a headbanger.

I'd never danced before. You'd think I would have, growing up in cafés, but no. Dancing's for girls. The idea that I could dance, that it was something I could do, that it was fun ... mental. I sort of jabbed the air and hopped about a bit. Everyone seemed to know what they were doing. I didn't have a proverbial. I'm sure I looked a right lemon. It didn't

19

matter. We were having fun. I was dancing to hippy noise and loving it.

That was my introduction to the real world. The realisation that a tiny part of my life could possibly be my own, that I could exist as an individual; massive. From then on things took off with Apollo 11. A door opened into a magic land of possibilities and ... oh, bliss ... there's actually something worth living for. Of course, it took a while to progress from there, to really *Going Out*. That truly was a *Giant Leap*. Me and the lads ventured forth from dilapidated churches, long forgotten by God or priest, to Saturday mornings at the Marquee and a hop and a moon-step to JoJo's.

Certain times in life are so supersonic, it's almost impossible to get the full bang of what they're about. Old Mother Nature starts pumping chemicals for the next delicious ancient rite of passage. The tribes need more foot soldiers to chase after the hairy mastodons. Raw sex energy explodes with the force of Bruce Banner changing into The Hulk, full of blood and guts. A dose of pulsating life shoves away the jaded childhood stage, allowing new roads to open up. It's time to join the big boys, play war games and dangle your wongle. I reckon the dance is all part of the same set-up. Music had to be part of an early-warning system with sound, vibrations, travelling over distance. Some bright ancestor having a laugh, playing around with shells, drums, whistles, and Bob's your first lookout. Then, after a good life-or-death hunt, what better way to celebrate than with some mind-bending substance, a bit of trance-dancing and getting down to round off the proceedings? Magic.

I do love wondering about things. There's a secret place in my head that no one knows about. Well, actually, I think Mr Easton might have a clue. Now and then in the past year he's been calling me the thinker or the philosopher. It goes over the other lads' heads, thank God, or I'd never live it down. Perhaps it comes from being in a set-up that has no time for family, friends, home life. Growing up in a café sounds different, exciting, and it is at times. It's also lonely, especially if you're a half-breed. Moving about makes you a gyppo. It's all you know. You learn to survive the best way you can. I disappeared into stories, lived with heroes, knights and ladies, bands of robbers living in wonderful woods, nice kids that were loved and went on adventures. Not bad really. Reality didn't stand a chance. The flip side is your brain goes wandering all over the shop and it never stops looking, asking, trying to make sense of all the insanity. Sometimes it drives me mad.

Along with the new self-pleasurable delights came something else. Hey ... that's almost a double entendre. I bet there's a name for it. Grammar's never been one of my concerns. If you read a book and like it, get the gist of it, who cares a toss if you don't understand all the clever words. Mind you, my vocab is growing, but I feel a bit weird if I stray into sounding poncey.

Anyway, the *something else* ... One day at school I walk into the gym, Christ knows why, probably getting out of some psycho's radar. There are these lads chucking a large orange ball about. The teacher spots me and says if you're coming in you've got to play. Funny how love affairs can come out of nowhere. I'm useless, of course, can't play for toffee and look a right twerp. The other guys are togged up in natty shorts with far-out, supersonic trainers. Thing is, they don't seem to mind I'm crap, show me the ropes and rules. Well that's it, job done. I'm in there every lunchtime, every one. It doesn't take long to get the hang of it, and like the dancing, it becomes my God. My real life has begun. Discos, basketball … what next? Happy days.

Sounds daft, but basketball's about learning to dance with your mates. Maybe all team sports are. After a while you learn the steps, the rules, and in time you're a fully fledged member of the gang. It's not an outside gang. You might not meet other than in the gym. In the dance you have your part to play, and it fits perfectly with all the others. If you don't fit right the whole thing falls apart. It's the first thing in the world I love. I learn everything about it. Spend hours training. I'd have slept there if they'd let me. I become pally with the lads in the team, and one of them, Matthew Drake, is into it as much as I am. After a while we click, and when we're on form there's a magic I can't explain. Don't want to. Why explain magic?

Reminds me of the three deaths … physics, chemistry, biology. All they do is break things down into the smallest bits until they vanish. They don't give a toss about the poor frog we dissect or the beautiful stones, the minerals we burn, and the lads go, 'Oooh, look at the sparks!' They're just things to use, dead, forgotten.

Bright sparks. Have a look at the bright sparks of Hiroshima; there's science for you. Mr Easton brought this box in last week, full of mementos, replicas, but they did the job. Letters from Japanese survivors, photos and that.

22

We read an article by some journalist called Hersey, who wrote about them. It was dark, real, had an effect inside your guts somewhere. What do scientists know? Those wallahs made the bombs and then called them *Fat Man* and *Little Boy*. What's that? What sort of sick, insane mind would do that? *Here, let's find some funny names to call these bombs that'll kill hundreds of thousands of people.* I bet they had a few laughs at that. I'd like to get hold of them and ask them how their *Little Kids* are. Wankers. Mr Easton has that effect on me. He goes mad about my grammar, structure. Says I might be a good writer … *If only.* I hate *If onlys.*

Basketball isn't an *If only.* It's my introduction to poetry. Yeah, poetry. When it works it sings like a naffing great diamond somewhere that makes sense of everything. It vanishes all the hate of Taras and dodging the mad psychos at school. It sends me to a place where there's nothing.

Seven

The change over the last couple of years is cosmic. The little kid's gone, the voice has deepened and I'm quite hairy, as it happens. Haven't started shaving yet, but you never know. Some lads look like apes. I don't envy them or the little geezers. Christ, you don't want to be a little geezer in our school, or a fat one, or a thin one who's poor and wears glasses. In fact, unless you're one of the hard nuts you don't want to be anything, but the trouble is there's a pecking order whether you like it or not. Even the top dogs have to keep looking over their shoulders. Horrible. I'd say I'm somewhere in the middle but there's no escape, *no keep your head down and nose clean*. Every day is a *Christians and Lions* day. You have a laugh, and some nutter whacks you. Do something stupid, and you get the cane.

Nightmare.

Off out tonight. Saturday ... best day of the week. Me and my mate Johnny are *The Funk Brothers*, into the same music, clothes, everything, but, unlike me, he never talks about his family, so I don't ask. Well, I might have done once and got the message. I don't think there's any agro, more your average zombies that are hard up, drink too much and die slowly watching naff TV. I hardly ever see his mother, and when I do, she looks well sad. Wanders about with a fag in her mouth that's been there for years. Some people seem to have this misery shadow stuck to their bodies. The father's morphed into his stain-encrusted armchair, an alien out of *Doctor Who*.

I don't know why people stay together. Perhaps it's because they fancied each other to begin with and after a while it wears off. By that time they're stuck, hate each other's guts and can't stand the idea of being alone. The only time they get along is when they're out of their heads, and that doesn't last. See them next day, you'd think someone's died.

Johnny's house is council, all greys and browns. Grey on the outside and shades of death brown on the inside. It stinks of cigarettes and has a limbo feel about it. Not that I've been anywhere apart from his room, which is poky, nothing much but his bed, cupboard and a couple of posters. He likes football, which I'm useless at, and supports Liverpool. For some reason I'm a Chelsea boy. I was about seven when I found out, something to do with the FA Cup Final. Didn't know a left-back from a right tit. I have heard these plums go on and on about facts and figures, get stuck in and chunter for hours about naff all. Thing is, I bet they don't even play, or if they do, they're as useless as I am. They have all the proper lingo: *toe-punt, inside foot, curler*. Only curlers they've ever known is their mum's.

Sometimes I can be a right prat.

It took a couple of years of basketball to lose the chubbiness of too many burgers and chips. The growth spurts in that

26

time, in all areas, are monumental. The explosions are not only of the seminal kind. The boat race gets peppered with lovely zits, and squeezing them becomes an art form in itself. They seem to miss some kids altogether. You start noticing these lovely faces that are unblemished. It's all part of the learning, I suppose. Notice one type of face, and you start seeing the differences, the shades of flesh. I love the pink-and-white smoothness some girls have that's marbled. It screams to be touched, kissed. Oh dear.

About this time there's a change in reading matter. My love affair with books started with thieving, born out of a childish desire to get away with something, a pathetic sense of power. Not having any dosh to waste on anything but a few sweets meant learning new tricks. I'd walk past second-hand shops that sold all sorts of tat, and they'd have tables with bits and pieces outside. I'd put my duffel coat on top of a book, pretend to be having a gander, then lift the coat with a book as well. Naughty boy. Oh, the thrill of getting away with something; dangerous beginnings. With the passing of two years I'd gone from Enid Blyton to pulp fiction to *Mayfair*, courtesy of the old man's secret stash. It takes a lot of guts to steal, enjoy and return … unblemished … Taras's forbidden articles. Happy days.

Familiarity and overindulgence dulls the excitement factor and leads to a demand for more bounce. I don't know where the line is between natural hormonal experimentation in puberty and excessive sexual addiction, but there must be a graph somewhere that skyrockets. The thing about addiction is it's two sides of a desperate coin. One is the thrill and the other is the fear. After a while there's as much fun from the desire to be found out as the addiction itself. One sin spawns another.

The secrets are coming thick and slimy. I've noticed a change in the lads at school, which must be to do with similar experiences. There's less giggling about bints and more eyeing them up with a desperation in the eyes. The talk is not so much of childish impossibilities and more a sharing of who's done what with who. There's still hype and bravado chucked in the mix but with a growing sense of expectation, of joining a higher level.

Then there's the fashion and styles, all part of the same changing landscape, a natural movement from one adulteration to the next. I love the way words are connected yet seem to slip and twist into other meanings. *Adulteration* obviously comes from the root *adult,* and yet it means *to make (something) worse by adding something to it.* Becoming a grown-up is a process of becoming worse. Common knowledge. Love it.

With all these bubbling volcanoes and initiations comes a move to the next dance platform. *JoJo's.* The first thing that hits you when you enter this adolescent emporium is the buzz. It's still for kids, no alcohol, but there's nothing here that ain't glam. The second is that it's a *night* club. No daytime kiddies here. Most of the staff are only a couple of years older than me, and the geezers that own it are invisible. At this point I haven't a clue about all the ins and outs, all I'm after is the dancefloor.

The togs start off a bit haphazard. Straight Levi's after sitting in the bath. Psychedelic shirts that make you look a right gimp, and any old shoes. Trouble is, when you're changing gear from one stage to the next, there's often a cash-flow problem. It starts to be important in a way it never was. I've done alright for a normal fifteen-year-old. Mum always chucks a few quid my way, especially as I work quite a bit behind the counter of whatever business we've got going, but it never amounts to much on the streets. A fiver doesn't go far after a packet of Marlboros, the entrance to JoJo's and a drink, so I start nicking as much as I can to supplement my needs. It's quite easy when you've got a till full of dosh. After a while I have plenty of geld. The risk I'm taking is phenomenal. If Taras ever found out, I'd be dead meat. Another little secret for one of my boxes.

Fashion is happening. It doesn't give a monkey's about the unemployment figures or the miners' strike. Seems to give two fingers to all that. Here it is, clear as day. Boutiques popping up all over the shop. My Arab mates are the ones to watch. They have the style because they have the money. I know I'm half one myself, but they really don't make themselves popular with the Brits. They don't work, have the best birds, best clothes, cars, gaffs and look alright, mostly. Especially the Libyans. Saudis are a bit dark, hairy and lairy. They think they're God's gift with the oil and lay the Aramis on a bit thick; makes me wonder what they're trying to cover up. What I find hilarious is the religion bit, seeing as Muslims are supposed to pray five times a day, be teetotal and no sex until you're hitched. Ones I know do everything. Apart from pray.

Eight

A while back Mr Easton was ill and they got some old geezer to cover. If I'd known beforehand I would have bunked off. The old git was nice enough, waiting for his pension in a year or so. The lads gave him hell. After a nightmare half-hour trying to settle everyone, he finally gets their attention, sort of, opens a book and recites:

> Awake! for Morning in the Bowl of Night
> Has flung the Stone that puts the Stars to Flight:
> And Lo! the Hunter of the East has caught
> The Sultan's Turret in a Noose of Light

Let's just say the lads were not impressed, obviously. The barrage of paper planes and abuse that lands on the poor geezer might have given him a hint. They couldn't care less about poetry, and I don't blame them. It's all lah-di-dah and airy-fairy. The rich wallahs and weirdos of the clever brigade have not a clue what living is about down in the gutters and sewers of the streets. How they expect kids like us to make sense or even care about poetry, Shakespeare, all the arty-farty stuff, is incredible. Most of the lads are happy with *The Beano*, some have moved on to Marvel comics and *The Sun* (for page three and the sports). Last week we had another poetry lesson. Step up Easy Easton and watch the difference.

'World War Three, boys, any takers?' I love this man and always go with his flow. I actually wish he was my dad, but maybe that's too weird. I stick my hand up, not knowing what I'm about to say. Impulsive? Far-out loony tune, man.

'Ah, the thinker awakes! Mr Al-Yawer.'

'The chances of us blowing everything to pieces is on the back burner at the moment, sir, but the cowboys are doing a good job in Vietnam.'

'Thank you, Naseem. Anyone else? Anyone know how many nuclear weapons are around?' Various answers from 'My dad's got one in the shed, sir' to 'Hundreds' and even a 'Forty-seven'.

'Thank you, thank you, thank you … and the correct answer, gentlemen and gentlemen is … drumroll, please.' The lads respond in lemming style, and the whole class is banging their desks. Easy Easton lets it thunder and brings out his megaphone from his desk and gives the honk. The noise dies down and through the megaphone he whispers, 'Forty-one thousand, five hundred and sixteen, and that's just an estimate. Each one of these bombs can destroy a whole city. What's that got to do with poetry? Nothing, absolutely nothing. Let's get rid of the word *poetry*, because it stinks to high heaven like a nuclear bomb. Let's invent something here and now that is our own. Anyone?' Again the usual trite attempts at humour.

'How about *Crap*? How about life, death and the crap … and magic of existence? Michael, what did you do this weekend that was different from every other weekend, every other day?' Innuendos in varying degrees of explicitness fill the air.

'Come on, please, one thing that made you excited.'

'I had a go in my dad's Cortina up the rec, sir. Nearly killed someone. Dad managed to reach across and put his foot on the brake. Gave me a right slap, sir. I hate the plank. Sorry, sir.' Riotous laughter. Michael Braithwaite is a gentle giant. Funny without trying to be.

'Excellent, Michael. How did it feel? Not the slap, the experience of driving?'

'Awesome, sir. I was doing alright, until little Jim Spelling popped out of nowhere. For a moment I thought I'd helped him on his way.'

'Good word, Michael, *Awesome*. The word comes from the old English word *Awe* and means something amazing, extraordinary, something that inspires fear, wonder. Okay, let's put it up there. Tell me, Michael, what felt awesome?'

'The power, sir.'

'Good, excellent. Anyone else? Come on, lads, help me out.' I jump in with 'revving guts' and someone else shouts 'manic wheels', and everyone's getting it and adding as Easy Easton writes it all on the blackboard, and pretty soon, we have a mishmash of absolute rubbish that looks great but means nothing. He gets Michael up and asks him to start a sentence with one of the words and then another lad and another, and we end up with:

33

The awesome power
of revving guts,
screech in the wreck
and crash.
Inside the hood
the bonnet snaps,
as manic wheels
spin out, explode.
Death driver,
moans in thunder,
slams the brakes
while rubber burns
spins out and rolls
the sirens wail.

Easy Easton ... magic.

Nine

The clock's on five, and Stevie Mack's fouled out with Danny Glazier on. Danny's a defender, okay on a good day, but he's so slow because of his height: his brain takes time to register what he needs to do. The *shiny boys* are on form, and we've got a six-point deficit. Their defence is solid, and we're not breaking their formation. We need something different, and our coach is not up to it. I call time-out with four and a half minutes left.

'What's up, Naz?' Mr Wendel, our basketball coach, is trying to look angry, annoyed, but he doesn't cut it. 'That's our last time-out gone. I told you to leave it to me. Never mind, gather round. They've got this sewn up unless we keep to the plan. Michael, all you've got to do is lose number four and get down under the basket. Naz or Matthew will feed you on the break. Danny, I need you to be one-on-one on their scorer; he's on form and cannot be allowed to shoot from anywhere near the zone. Stick to the half-court press and look for the break. They'll make a mistake, and we need to be there. Alright, get out there and get those points.'

Wendel's straight as a die. He can't think out of the ordinary, and we're going to lose. I grab hold of Matthew and Michael, give them my plan. They look at me like I'm mental but know I'm able to deliver, so they agree. I get Michael to swap with Danny and one-on-one their star player, number eight, and tell Tom Ansell, our pivot, to float at their end line. He looks at me, laughs as the ref starts the game. They've got possession and play it safe, keeping out of range.

Sometimes you've got to draw a foul if you want to change the flow of the magic. Sometimes you need a miracle. Sometimes a bit of cunning and pushing the limits. I catch up with Matthew who's onto one of their guards with the ball, and we rumble him. The ref blows a foul, they miss the shots, and it takes another thirty seconds off the clock. Wendel's screaming about staying on plan and I shout *forty-two*. The lads go into one-on-one and squeeze hard. The opposition goes into panic, and I shout *seventeen*. Whoever's got the ball is attacked by the three closest to him, and he fumbles. Charlie's gone berserk down the right, I've got the ball, lob it to the end zone, and he kills it.

Three minutes left, and I shout *forty-two* again, and we hassle them to drop it in their own half. They're defending well, but Charlie's dribbling like a nutter. He leads his defender a merry dance and comes down the middle. We fake a couple, switch a couple, and it's in the bag. We need two baskets. They call their last time-out. It's getting a bit rough out there, and there are two minutes left.

'Naz, I told you to keep to the plan. What the hell are you doing?'

36

'We're doing it, sir. It's the only way. There's no time for defence and strategy, we've got to hit them sneaky, fast.' I'm being loud-mouthed and lairy. It's what I do best. Someone has to.

'Alright, it's working,' Wendel said, 'but we need two baskets. Michael's our best bet. He doesn't miss, and they can't reach him once he's under the basket. I want a four-man defence with Michael floating.' The whistle goes, and we're out there.

Matthew comes up to me and says, 'There's no time, Naz.'

'I know. Listen, forget Wendel. They're going to play for time. We need to hassle from the go. You with me? He'll blow a fuse, probably suspend us from the next game.'

He didn't need to say anything. We slap hands and head to work. They start the game, and I whisper one-on-one to the lads. The clock's ticking, and the shiny brigade are doing well keeping the ball. I hustle their main man who's showing me his dribbling skills and being a right ponce. I manage to snatch the ball; I'm away for two, levelling it. They'll probably try for extra time as they look knackered and the wind is on our side. Wendel's screaming to stay tight, and the ref tells him to keep it down.

They take the play and pass it around half-heartedly. My ticker's beating ten times faster than the clock, and I look at Charlie, nod for him to float. They get a shot in, and Michael's up there with the rebound, hammers it to Matthew, who's found space, and it looks like it's over when he's taken down. Ref calls a foul with ten seconds left. A fight nearly breaks out; the ref has to talk to the trainers. Wendel tells me to take the free shots. I miss them both. I naffing miss them both, but six-foot-two Danny Glazier, Danny the sloth, Danny the beanpole – *which way are we shooting, lads?* – rebounds, grabs the ball and, after three goes with three defenders hacking him to pieces, scores. Two seconds left on the clock. Killer supersonic, man. Outta sight.

The shiny boys are sad all over in the dressing room. It happens that way, someone wins, someone loses. We call them *shiny boys* because of their outfits, natty, expensive tops and shorts with names and numbers in silky fabric and bright colours. They're nice kids, mixed Catholic school, grammar. I hate them. Mad, innit? The hate of the tribes. I like to think I'm different, but I'm not. The psycho stuff runs in the blood. We're all a mixture of the vomit that's been passed down, handed along with the blood. Here, take this, it's all yours, it's who you are. This wally's your dad, and here's your old dear. Choice? Naff off. Have some of that and all, blonde, brunette, big nose, ugly-pugly, handsome git, as thick as a plank or bright as a button. It comes from your genes and a bit of social sciences, economics, history, geography and the British Empire. Nuts to the lot of them.

One of the shiny lads looks well hard and keeps giving me the stare. He and his shorter mate with the crewcut and skin as fair as a girl's are the top dogs of their team. They're good but have no edge. They play like lords, gentlemen, and probably have wealthy parents who lavish their spawn with love and attention. There's an air about money that makes people walk different, talk different. Fart different.

'Hard luck, chaps. Thought you had it for a while. Tickety-boo, what?' When my blood's up I find it hard not to niggle; it's not good. It's the plank coming out trying to push the line and start something. Why? Why not enjoy life as it is? Why's that not enough? Why not be humble and really say something nice? There's a knee-jerk attack mode that's sad, selfish, comes from pain. Anyone who's got money, nice parents, nice clothes, a kind nature … slag them. The poison has to come out and eat some flesh. I'll end up more twisted than Taras if I'm not careful.

They don't say anything and wander off with their heads down. Wendel comes in and says *Well done!* and other useless rubbish. He tries to make out he was in on the play and what a magnificent team effort it all was. All in all, he's okay really and has made the team what it is, but there's nothing left for him to give. His arsenal's limited.

'Third in the league, lads, third. All we need is to play like today, and the cup's in the bag. I am so proud of you boys,' he said and walked out swinging his whistle on its long string, cock of the hoop. He likes to think he owns us.

'He don't half talk mush,' said Charlie, coming out of the showers looking red as a tomato. The changing room's filling up with steam. Other lads are flicking wet towels at each other and screaming abuse.

'He's alright,' I said. 'I think we need someone else, though. It was a good game.'

We walk out of school together chatting about the game, and as we pass the main building get jumped on by four of the shiny boys. With the speed and surprise of it we don't stand a chance. They're taking a risk so close to the school, but it's after hours and no one's about. They drag us into a green area by the side of the building with high hedges and some trees. Me and Charlie are not useless and give as good as we get, but the odds are too high. We're getting thrashed when Danny and Mike turn up, and the shiny boys leg it, laughing. Even nice kids have monsters inside. The lads wanted to give chase, but I'm not up for it. Too tired from the game, and somehow, inside, I feel I deserved it.

Ten

'Be ready in ten minutes.' Johnny's mother's voice has nothing to it. It doesn't say anything about who she is. It's flat, empty, a sort of monotonous grey. Johnny's brushing his teeth. He's always brushing his teeth, Christ knows why. I hardly brush mine at all. Well, that's not true, but it's not something I've been brought up to think of as important … so dentures by the age of thirty here I come.

'Have you done them enough?'

'Least they're all mine. Well, king tosser, you let the shiny boys *kick yo' honky ass, bro. That is so sad, man.*' The JB's are on with 'Gimme Some More', and we both start giving it fly, which is hard in Johnny's room, but we do it in style. Fred Wesley's sax is eating up the blues and laying it down super-thick, gloopy-funk honey.

After a while I jump on his bed, look through *The Sun.* Johnny's not interested in much other than footy and the scene. He's not bothered about school and already lining up restaurant jobs. Wants to be a waiter. Reckons they're up there with the funk. According to him, once you've done your apprenticeship you get decent dosh, the birds love you and everyone looks up to you. It must be nice knowing what you want to do.

'Why didn't you go in today?' I ask.

'Went to see about the job. Starting next week.' He's playing it down like it's no big deal, but I know he's been after this for ages. Johnny's mum and dad are skint; he's been dreaming of the day he'll have a bit of wonga since forever.

'What you doing?' He's stopped brushing the teeth and is on to the toenails, sitting on the end of his bed, cutting them with a deep intensity, dropping the nails on the carpet.

'Kitchen staff basics you have to start off with unless you do a waiting course. I'm not doing that, man. I'll be moving up the ranks like a dose of diarrhoea.'

'Urgh, don't, mate. Specially not in a restaurant.'

'They want more staff if you're interested. I can ask, if you like,' he said and started on the hair, looking in the mirror on the inside of his wardrobe.

'What's going on, Johnny, you going somewhere on a promise? You haven't stopped with the grooming lark. Who is it and why haven't you told me?'

'No, man. It's the restaurant ... they want me in tonight to have a look around, watch how it's done.' He shuts the wardrobe door and sits down on his bed.

'Well?' he says.

'What?'

'Shall I ask about a job?'

'Yeah, why not.' I'm not keen, but it might be something to help me get out from under Taras and his tyranny. Johnny slams the volume up, and we're up again and giving it grief to James Brown. The door opens and there's Johnny's mum. She's four foot nothing, round as a barrel, thick-rimmed glasses and pink curly hair. She's so taken a back she stands there for a few seconds not knowing what to say.

'Turn that noise down, John, and come down for tea.' We take no notice and keep with the groove.

'Come on, Mrs Hatton, shake your money-maker.' I grab her hand and bring her into the room and keep dancing. Johnny's cracking up, and I'm getting up close and hot with the vibes.

'No, no … stop it, Naseem, please. Peter will be up here in a minute and have a heart attack.' It's the first time I've seen a smile on her face. She's like a little girl. She pulls away, turns to look at us. 'So this is what you boys get up to. It's wicked.' She's giggling as she goes downstairs. 'Now come on, Johnny, it's getting cold.' Johnny and me look at one another and crease up.

'I'd better go,' I say and grab my rucksack, heading downstairs. Johnny comes after me. 'I'll see you in town tomorrow about ten in Churchill Square,' I say and shout goodbye to his mum.

Eleven

'You can't be serious, Naz, that shirt is bonkers. It's so hippy dippy, man. Paisley has to be subtle, man, unless you're heading for Yes or Pink Floyd.' Saturday in Brighton is always heaving. We're in WH Smith's checking out the singles, and he's having a right go. The shirt is bright reds and mauves, satin, with a teardrop collar and ruffle sleeves. I don't know why he's going on ... well, I do actually. Sometimes you buy something you know is naff, but you do it anyway. Besides, I'm wearing my blue seersucker jacket on top, so it hardly shows. There's a pretty bint smiling at our conversation, and I check her out, smile back to let her know I've sussed she's listening.

'You don't half talk turkey, man. This shirt is wild, it's happening, it's laying down the style.' I put it on a bit for her, she laughs, pretends to go and do something further off. Johnny clocks my brain and dead arms me.

'Lay off the beams, man, it's so uncool.' I grab the headphones on the music counter and take no notice of him. I start dancing, dancing for her, the whole naffing shop. I get the usual looks from the punters. Nutter? I'm in the groove, daddy. Johnny creases up and leaves as if he's not with me as I start to sing. I'm singing 'Heaven Must Have Sent You', by The Elgins.

Some songs you recognise as soon as they start even though you've never heard them before. That's mad, right? It's like I know them from some other life. You can look at a killer song from all over, and it's perfect. I reckon that's what Mr Easton means when he goes on about writing. He says everything can be like that. Wish I could say the same about my singing. Trouble with singing with headphones on is you sound a right wally to everyone else. The old biddies buying their Mills and Boon paperbacks give me some well grumpy stares. Anyway, the bint seemed to like it, she and her mate behind the counter are giggling away. Some misery guts must have told the manager. I see him strolling over with the face on and give it a rest.

'Yeah, I'd like this one please, miss.'

'That'll be 50p, please,' She's still smiling but trying to be straight up.

'Do you like my singing?' I lean across the counter all serious.

'I thought you weren't feeling well.' Cheeky mare. Hey, when you're on a roll, press it home.

'You busy tonight?'

'Here's your change and your receipt, and yes, I'll be with my boyfriend.'

'Can he dance?'

'Not bad. Was there anything else, sir?' She flicks her long brown locks and stands all prim. She is enjoying it,

I can tell; a tiny smile is trying to form, but she keeps it back.

'Not bad? That says it all really. So where are you being busy tonight? I only ask because I noticed you were watching me. How serious is it with the geezer? I bet you can dance. No, listen, I can tell by looking at people's body shapes. There's a certain way dancers stand and move, even when they're not dancing. Straight up, I know what I'm talking about. I'm into funk, James Brown, soul stuff ... I bet you like the Chi-Lites.'

The boss moves in next to me; he's been standing a few feet away, ready to pounce.

'Is everything okay, Sharon?'

'Oh yes, Mr Boughton.'

'Sharon's been very helpful. Thanks, Sharon, I'll see you tonight at JoJo's. Cheerio, Mr Boughton.'

Johnny's smoking outside. I grab his fag and take a toke.

'You're losing it, Naz.'

'Never had it, Johnny.'

'I asked about the job. The boss said there might be something in a couple of weeks.' I'm quite relieved it's not happening soon, if ever. The reality of having to actually graft needs to be put well away. Not that I'm lazy. I know it's coming, but my brain needs time to adjust.

'What we up to?' I ask to change the subject.

'I'm playing footy this afternoon. I'll see you tonight.' Johnny's upset about something. I think his dad's on the way out. Smokes too much, been in and out of hospital this last year. He doesn't help himself, won't stop, reckons it's too late.

Twelve

I walk home eyeing up the bints, play a few games of table football with Beejan, one of the regular punters, then head up to my room to relax. My room's on the second floor. It's tiny, and like all the rooms of my acquaintance, manky. Whenever we've moved, which has been quite a few times, it's always to somewhere cheap and nasty. I can understand that. Times are hard, the family's on the lowest rung, but home has never been anything other than forgotten rooms above a business of some sort. It's exactly like other foreigners. The money areas are tarted up for punters but the rest of the place is a doss house. Take a look at the upstairs windows of any takeaway establishment and you'll have a hint of what the rest of the house is like. Dirty lace curtains hide the mystery within.

I'm on my bed reading when I hear mum's dulcet, nasal tones calling me.

'Naseem, I need you to be here while I go to the doctor's with Jamal.' Mum's stressed, looks gaunt. The make-up's a bit splashed on, and she's chain-smoking.

'When are you going?' I ask.

'Ten minutes. Your father's in bed asleep, don't disturb him.'

'What's wrong with Jam?' Mum's getting ready to go, and her mind's not on the spot.

'He's got a fever. I shouldn't be long, just don't do anything stupid,' she says and heads upstairs. I was going to say *like what?* but leave it, go downstairs and start chopping up some onions. I make a monster burger with salad, pickles, dressing, sit behind the bar and chat with Beejan. He gazes at my burger with a sad look on his mug, so I give him half.

Beejan's a bit slow. Not stupid but not that bright. Loves the café and spends most of his life here. I don't know how he survives. He's never got any money even though he does under-the-counter cleaning jobs. He's in his early twenties, acts more like fifteen. He's a sort of café mascot, and ... have a laugh ... the old man really likes him. So do I, as it happens. We share a love of the dance, the scene. He lives in a bedsit the size of a wardrobe and eats tons of rice because it's cheap. Maybe that's why he's not small.

'Naseem, brother, when we hitting the town again, man? We haven't for so long, Naz. I'm missing it.' He tucks into the burger and leaves some around his mouth. I give him a tissue and get us a couple of Cokes.

'Going out tonight, Beejan.'

'Where?'

'JoJo's. Fancy it?' His face turns sour. Beejan's one of those people you can read by their faces. What he thinks comes up like a road sign.

'Banned, brother. They say I never buy anything, bloody English. I pay the entrance fee, what matter if I don't buy drinks? It because I take my own water bottle.' I try and explain the ethics of business as mum comes down the stairs with Jamal, who looks his usual petrified state and they head off to the doctor's. About an hour later the old man comes down accompanied by death. You'd think they'd give each other a rest now and then, but I suppose that's what good friends are for, always together.

'Mr Al-Yawer, I beat you at football if you fancy it?' Beejan has no idea of the niceties of atmospheric energies. Taras walks past him without blinking, makes himself a black coffee, goes outside to smoke.

'What's the matter with your dad, Naz?'

'He's got cancer.'

'No, man! You're joking.'

'No. I'm praying.'

It's all over Beejan's head. He's nearly crying as I explain I really am joking.

'It's not nice to joke like that, Naseem.'

I put some money in the jukebox and sit there with Beejan, playing draughts. He lights up, and I take a few tokes of his fag. He thinks it's really naughty and keeps turning around, checking the front window on the lookout for Taras.

'He good man, your dad. Like my father. Very strict. Is much better than English. They don't love their children, Naz. They don't care about God or anything. They don't care, brother.'

'Yeah, but you like getting friendly with their daughters, Beejan.' He cracks up and goes on about his troubles.

'I want to marry, Naseem, but I can't find right one. My father's coming to see me next month ... I want to have a

nice girlfriend to show him his son is doing well, you know?'
Taras is talking to someone outside. There's something not
right about it, the way it's moving, there's an urgency of
motion and the talk is changing pitch. Beejan clocks it and
gets up to hear what's going on.

'Naz, man, it's Muftah, that madman. Better call police,
quick.' Beejan's sweating; he does that when he bricks himself
for whatever reason. Outside the talk is getting ugly. Muftah
is a heavy who's known for being psychotic. The cops are
after him for various activities, but he's too sharp for them.
What he and the old man have in common is beyond me. It
might be something to do with Helen, a young woman who
works in the café a few hours at weekends. I think Muftah is
trying to get her involved in his shady dealings.

Then I see something that catches me off-guard. I love it
when that happens. Moments when all the ordinary and the
known fall away and you see something that wakes you up,
even if it's only for a few seconds. Taras grabs this geezer that
has a reputation for violence by the scruff of his jacket, walks
him like a schoolboy. He stands there as Muftah picks himself
up from the street where he's landed.

'Is this how it's going to be, Abu Naseem?'

The old man tells him to get lost in no uncertain terms,
and he does, mumbling something under his breath. After
a few seconds, Taras comes in, smiles at Beejan, asks if he
wants to play table football.

Funny old game.

Thirteen

It's all snake stuff this growing up; you don't need that Freud geezer to know it's all about sex. Everything. Look at the papers, the mags, the books. *The Joy of Sex*. It's everywhere, progressive and that. Everyone's *exploring* themselves and having a right laugh until the party's over. Oh dear. Things look so normal in daylight, but come the night and everything changes. I reckon that's where the vampire myths come from. Ordinary people who turn into ravenous sex fiends when the sun goes down.

I meet Johnny by the Clock Tower, and we nip round to this swanky pub that's crammed. Only reason we go there is to waste a bit of time before JoJo's, plus they have this fruit machine that always pays out but you need to really put all your magic on to it. I'm wearing black velvet loons with a massive flare, red leather platforms, a tight white T-shirt and some bangles. I tell mum the Libyan boys give me their old togs, hand-me-downs. Lies. Easy as pie. You play the game and your nose doesn't get any longer. Love it.

Nine o'clock we head off. It's still light. The sky's got that softness, the air is warm and the beats of our hearts are buzzing. Everyone's out. This is my town, and I love it. It's mad, sometimes dangerous, but it's happening. Johnny's looking the business wearing my light-blue flares, black shirt open at the front and black shoes with a bit of heel on them. The shoes are naff, but he hides them under the flares. He's got a light, fake-gold chain to finish things off. His mousy brown hair's a bit long and limp; he has this way of tossing his head to keep the straggly bits off his face. He's looking sharp.

So here we are in JoJo's ... no shuffling here. The Motown's minimal, for skinheads and suedies; old hat. Living in the past and holding on to something that's dead. Us boys are the colour of the times, and that colour, my friends, is Funk. The Godfather, James Brown, rules the sound waves, followed by a deluge of black brothers and one or two honkies who lay down the golden tracks. There's Isaac Hayes, Junior Walker, Al Green and then there's a deeper level. That's where we are and it's home, a place you share with the few. They know, you know, and it's outta sight, man. It's being born out of a chrysalis, some alien birth that changes your vibrations. One minute you're a spotty kid that laughs at silly jokes, next you're a brother that's hip and funky.

The pop stuff is good in places, Bowie, Glitter, T. Rex, with different styles happening all over the shop. In the beginning we didn't have a clue, danced to anything until our socks stank. After a while things change without you noticing. You look to the older lads and start to see something, the beginnings of a moving towards it. It grabs you when you're not looking, and that's it. With dancing, there's a right way and a toss way and your body starts to know the difference. After a lot of heartache, practice, you find the dance, or maybe it finds you. It seeps into your skin and bones.

There's a dancing that's up there near to heaven. A place of power, vanishing, a strength that comes from giving it all. The bint-chasing comes second, no, maybe third after your brothers. You're always on the lookout for skirt, never know your luck, but the life of the dance is the dance of life, and the dance is funk. In time you get better, but there are always those up ahead who've made a name for themselves, and if you're lucky they let you hang around, join their circle. With all this there's the danger, it never leaves. You learn to live with it. You might be in paradise, but it has a price.

Stay on the scene, like a sex machine! The boys are in a line doing it to death. We've been dancing for about an hour non-stop, sweat soaking the shirts, faces dripping. The place is packed with terrific-looking bints, and yes, Sharon's here … and man, oh man, can she dance. Togged in tight red flares and a purple top that hugs nicely. She's with some mates that are well tasty.

We move nearby but don't crash them, it's not the way. They've got to give the signs, the vibes; it's all secret lingo. After a while, you're speaking without speaking. Even though we chatted earlier it doesn't mean anything, not here on the floor. It's another dimension where bodies and eyes do the business. I have a rest, and Sharon comes over, we smile at the same time.

'Where's the boyfriend?'

'There isn't one.'

'Sorry about earlier.'

55

'It was funny. You're funny. I'm Sharon.'

'I know. I'm Naz. Smoke?'

So it goes. I love this bit. It's all jive that trickles off the tongue like rain down a gutter. I can do it blindfold. It's the next bit … no … the bit after that; the next bit's obvious. You dance, get close, kiss and … then … that bit. I hit a wall every time.

There are two worlds, well … there are probably loads, but listen up. There's the world of the dance, the night, chasing skirt, and then there's the day. You have to keep them separate. If you get serious, it's over. The days and nights become one big mess, and that's you fixed, old son, the road to hell. Couple of years, get engaged, naff job to build up the savings on a down payment and guess what? You're as dead as your mum and dad. Nah. I'm not doing it, man. This is the decade of decadence, my friend. As Mr Easton says, it's cyclical, comes with depression, economic, social upheavals, usually before a major war. Happy days.

Sharon's well up for it, shares a flat with two of her mates and wants to take me home. Funny how you think you're after something so bad and when it's served up, you're not hungry. I make some half-cocked excuse about having to meet someone, but it doesn't wash. She changes straight away and goes back to her mates. Ten minutes later she leaves, walking past like I'm not there. It's not like this in the films … well, maybe it is.

'What happened, man?' Johnny's got the hump. He was doing alright with one of Sharon's mates.

'Don't know, think they were having a laugh.' I don't like lying to Johnny. It does something inside that's not good. My mood changes, and I stop dancing.

'You alright, Naz?'

'Yeah, man, I'm cool. Need a breather. Fancy a Coke?'

I go outside and light up a fag. Car horns are blaring, having a row, and some seagulls are doing the same, digging at bin bags across the street. It's a clear night with a few stars, and I'm wondering if there's something wrong with me. There's a big deal about losing your virginity that becomes this nightmare hanging over everything. All us lads go around giving it the rabbit, but there's a blank look on our faces that can't be disguised. None of us have done it. Reminds me of those baboons that wander about in packs trying to look hard but it's all bluff. Hoo … Hoo … Hoo … Who's going to be the first out of our lairy gang? I think old Siggers would say I'm building up to a complex. Christ knows.

When I go back in, Johnny's dancing a slow one with Sandra. He catches my eye and nods in a certain direction. I look over and see this girl eyeing me up, but it's not blatant, she blushes as I catch her gaze and turns away. I'm not feeling very hip after bottling it with Sharon and wonder if I need to leave it, keep to myself, but something makes me walk over and sit next to her. I offer her Johnny's Coke, and she takes it. She's lovely, not in a sexy way, not wanting a shag. We start chatting, I can't remember what about, but it was different. I wasn't giving it all the blag and the fear in my guts had gone.

We move to a little alcove away from the music, and all the while I'm wondering what's going on in my head. The brain's a mental nightmare with all the different bits of who you are that come out to play and stick their oar in. Is that everyone or just me? I think I'm still reeling a bit from Sharon.

Her name's Abigail. She sees I'm a bit out of it, asks if I want to see her again, and I say, *Yeah, of course*. At turfing-out time, she gets picked up by this huge black limo. Oriental-looking geezer steps out and opens the door for her. Johnny comes over from snogging Sandra in the shadows. Sandra's mad keen on Johnny, a bit eager, if you know what I mean. She thinks he's sliced bread and he's not that bothered.

'Far out, man. She one of the royals? Any luck?' He's got the smile on but makes out he hasn't.

'Naff off.' I don't want him to see how pleased I am.

'She's well into you, man.'

'Leave it out, Johnny. Get back to Sandra.'

Johnny laughs. 'I love you, mate. Me and you, blood brothers, I know where you're at, it's cool, man. Catch you later, Nazzy.' He shimmies a bit and swans off.

Makes me smile.

Fourteen

My Arabic name ... you would not believe the grief it's given me, but I quite like it now. It's like Ziggy Stardust, *He was the Naz, with God-given ass*. I won't tell you my full name, you wouldn't be able to pronounce it, not properly. Most Brits haven't a clue what it's like to be different, not really. Everyone's tarred with the same hate. All Arabs are dodgy. I know tons of nice ones, as it happens, but my dear old dad ain't one of them. I avoid him as much as I can after crossing the line; he does the same. It doesn't change anything; the job's been done. Hate and fear don't just vanish, they twist and lurk about inside, somewhere in your guts. If you live with a poison long enough it takes you over. Maybe it's animal. Big dogs bite small dogs who bite smaller dogs, and for a while I become like Taras, my worst nightmare. I put that well away in my mental box, so far down I sometimes forget it's there. Funny old game.

The times are frazzled. There's so much happening. A million roads and not enough time, energy, to go down each one. Somehow you manage to keep all the balls in the air, but it takes a lot of lying, stealing, doing things that eat you up and old Jiminy Cricket's saying *hold up*, but you close your lugs and get on with it. Without knowing it, or maybe you do, you turn into a right plum, but your mates are just as bad. What can you do? There are far worse nutters out there.

Next day I'm doing the laundry in the afternoon. I'm laundry boy. One of my jobs. All the soiled clothes of our family stuffed into three or four bin bags, and uncle Naz does the business. I don't mind. Laundries are interesting places. I usually do my best essays between watching weirdos, alkies, wild and whacky people, nice people, not so nice mental droogs and tumbling pants and socks. For some reason I can't get into the writing today, I can't string two words together. It's Abigail, she keeps popping into my bonce. I try not to think about her but it doesn't work.

Normally, I'd be flying with the subject Mr Easton's given us for this week's essay. Rebels. He's wasted on me and the lads, I swear he should be in some amazing school teaching top-notch kids that hang on to his every word. Instead, he has to deal with lads farting and gobbing at one another. The gobbing is no ordinary gobbing, mind you; it's an art form. You learn to gob over distance and in silence. Not easy. Then there's the passing of the dirty mag game. Then there's the passing abusive notes game. Even though I haven't done the work, I go in. Monday's my favourite day, double English in the afternoon.

Easy Easton stands there absolutely still, not saying a word while the lads chunter, and because he doesn't shout or ask for quiet, we all realise he's waiting and gradually we shut up. Silence.

'Anyone know anything about Jesus?' The way he says it, everyone looks around as if Jesus might pop in through the door. Mr Easton does that. You think he's this little guy with no power, and he smashes your expectations.

'Is it a trick question, sir?' William Bate is slithery. He's well off but keeps it quiet. A bit arty, well clever when it comes to ducking and diving out of harm's way. He and his cronies are *nice kids* that get bullied by horrible kids like me and the lads.

'No, William, nothing tricksy.' Silence. 'Okay, I'm going to give you a potted history of some chap we know very little about. He was a Jew who lived in the Middle East at a time when there were a lot of warring tribes and tremendous uncertainty. Life was hard. The Romans ruled with an iron fist and were ruthless. They gave the big jobs to their cronies in government who lorded it over the little people.'

'Nothing changes, sir,' says Phil Blake, wide boy who plays it hard.

'Maybe you're right, Philip. But hang on, there are stories going around about a coming messiah who'll save the Jewish people, and some other madman, John the Baptist, is in the desert, the wilderness, preparing the way for him. How many of you go to church?' Laughter and yells of 'Leave it out, sir.' 'My gran goes, sir.'

'Thank you, Stephen. There we are. Okay, forget about all the things you've heard, picked up. One of you, today, here and now … starts hearing voices in your head.' Matthew Drake chips in, in his usual attempt at the funnies. Matthew likes to clown about in a harmless way, always telling naff jokes, trying to impress with dreadful magic tricks. Suits him as he's almost a dwarf, a bit runty.

'Is anyone there?' he says.

'Thank you, Matthew Drake.' Mr Easton never gets annoyed and knows how to play the lads. Sometimes he laughs with us, sometimes he laughs at us but never maliciously. 'These voices are telling you things. Suppose you heard an actual voice in your head that wasn't your own, how would you feel? Today, we'd say you were suffering from some sort of mental illness. We'd send you to a psychiatrist, give you medication. Keep you under observation until the voices disappeared. The Inuit people of the Arctic, the Indians of America, the shamans, tribal people everywhere, have always communed with the spirit world.'

'Auntie Mabel does that, sir.'

'I'm talking about young men, not much older than you, going out into the wilderness by themselves, the deserts, the jungles, to speak with their ancestors, with nature spirits. When they came back, they were men, able to advise the tribe.'

'Jesus was a nutter,' someone shouts from the back.

'Exactly. That's what most people thought about him. They locked him up, tortured him, crucified him. Why? Because he dared to think differently. He dared to say something that went against the norm. So what's the lesson? Anyone?'

'English, sir.'

'Thank you, Charlie. People don't like different. The lesson is … nobody wants you to think for yourselves. It's too dangerous. You might change things.'

After class, Mr Easton gives me an extra exercise book.

'What's it for, sir?'

'Whatever you want.' He puts his tweed jacket on and picks up his brown leather briefcase; soft leather, looks expensive.

62

Always dapper is our English teacher, not ostentatious but smart. Groomed to look like he doesn't care, handsome in a quiet way. I wonder what wifey looks like.

'Is it homework?'

'It's any work you want. It could be bus work or walking work.'

'Is this because I didn't do the essay, sir?'

'No. It's because you *can*.'

I walk out the classroom into the dead corridors of our daytime prison. Johnny's there with Phil Blake. Phil's one of the gang, only it's not a gang, just schoolmates. Phil's bright, intelligent in a mature sort of way, he could get into university if he tried. Probably end up working in a bank.

'Well?' Phil's waiting for a morsel of something to latch on to, crack a joke with. He stands there, leaning against a wall, both hands in his pockets, as if he's holding his crown jewels.

'No detention. Gave me an exercise book.' Johnny's tie is about as small as a blue goldfish. The rest of it is hidden inside his shirt; even in school clothes he looks the business. He has a way of slouching that's well relaxed, as if he's at this party that's been going for hours.

'Is he after you, Naz?' Phil's always ready with the jokes. Well, I suppose we all are, but he revels in it.

'Naff off, Phil. He's alright.'

'Hey, Johnny ... Naz's got a schoolboy crush. That's what happens when there are no skirts about, it's well documented. Look at all the rich wallahs, politicians, priests. Same-sex schools.'

'Phil ...'

'What?'

'Get lost.'

He whacks me around the head and runs off, laughing. Johnny and me walk after him towards the dining hall. Through the reinforced windows that surround the inner playground, we can see the usual madness happening. Someone's knuckling someone in a corner, and they're screaming. Twenty lads are killing each other playing footy with a tennis ball on concrete, and there'll be cuts and bruises. Lads are reading sex books and giggling in the shade against a wall, and seagulls are dumping on anyone that might be beneath. Not a cloud today. There's a blue that makes you feel sick it's so real; best not to look too long. Dad Duncan, oldest teacher in the school and easiest to torture, is finishing his mackerel sandwich. He's being followed by a line of six urchins, imitating him, and he's none the wiser.

'What's for lunch?' I ask.

'Serious?' Johnny hardly eats. I've never seen him tuck into anything. Mind you, the dinners are pretty awful. 'What happened last night? I thought they were well up for it.' Here it is, the moment of truth.

'You'll go mental.'

'Go on.'

'I bottled it.'

'What? You having a laugh?'

'I bottled, Johnny.' My intestines are twisting around trying to find a way out of my stomach, but I have to be honest with my mate.

'Why, Naz?'

'I don't know. Maybe there's something wrong with me.'

'Nah. You're a plum, that's all. What about the other one?'

'Abigail. She's … nice … we …'

'What?'

'We … made a date.'

Johnny cracks up with belly laughs.

'What's wrong with that, you prat?'

'Nothing, Naz, that's nice.'

'Lay off, Johnny.' We stand in the corridor leaning against things with a strange silence between us. I try and break it.

'Have you and Sandra …?' I know they haven't, know he doesn't want to, but it's the best I can do at the moment.

'No, man. She wants to go steady.'

'And?'

'No way, man, I don't want that nightmare. I'd end up dead inside.'

Fifteen

Schooldays are a torture we do our best to avoid by bunking off, listening to records, wandering around town. If we have any money, we'll go down the King Alfred Sports Centre, play table tennis. There's always a risk of getting spotted by some plank who might dob you in, but these days we're not bothered. I think they prefer it when we do bunk off. I say *we*, but mostly it's me and Johnny. Last year there were still four of us: Johnny, Phil, Mickey and me.

Mickey's a dark horse, half something foreign but doesn't say much about it. That's the thing with this growing up business, nobody says anything straight up. It filters down the back alleys if you need to know and all the rest is shtum. I reckon he's ashamed of being foreign. Maybe that's one of the reasons he keeps quiet, there's been a lot of agro in the last few years. Racist nutters out for blood. Out of the four of us, Mickey's the most stable. A good family makes all the difference.

It's Wednesday, the day of living death. Double trigonometry this afternoon, and they've got some poor tosser covering Barmy Arnold. Arnold's a sadist. He's having his gall bladder removed, and we all pray it kills him. Arnold's been trained by the Gestapo. No one dares muck about in his class, even us older lads toe the line. All except Billy Brannigan, a sixth former, who's number-one psycho. You wouldn't believe it to look or speak to him, comes across as a real nice geezer. Family's rolling in it. Billy always wears top gear, even his school blazer's bespoke. I chat to him every now and then if we bump into each other on the scene. He's not a mate, but someone to keep on the right side of. One day Barmy was having a mare about behaviour and got us all in the corridor standing in silence. Thirty lads in a line not daring to breathe too loud and Barmy's mouthing off. Around the corner comes Billy, clocks what's happening and walks casually behind him, taps his shoulder and, as he turns, headbutts him, walks away as if nothing's happened.

Well, as Barmy's being cut up, we bunk off to celebrate. The four of us head down to Portslade, slip quietly into the Mile Oak pub. Molly, the landlady, is a nice old dear who lets anyone in as long as you keep your nose clean. We buy a couple of Cokes, play pool and darts.

'Why are you boys not at school?' She's quite mumsy is Molly, likes to have us around. 'Look, there're some cheese and tomato sandwiches going stale here. I was going to give them to Larry.' Larry's a blind Staffie who's about ninety. He's got no hair and all these strange growths dangling from his body. Lovely dog, though, licks you till he's sick.

Molly has a way of laughing for no reason. It's a high-pitched cackle that starts and ends abruptly. She says a couple of words and laughs in between, even though it's not funny. 'Your last year, eh boys?' (Hysterical laughter.) 'I bet you can't wait.' (And again.) 'No more bunking off, you'll be free as little sparrows.' (Once more for luck.) Mad as a fruitcake. She's alright for an old dear, not that old really, fifty-odd? Reckon she's got a thing for young lads.

Phil does his bit, he's a right performer at heart. 'Bunking orf? Actually, madam, I'll have you know we're undertaking a survey of local establishments in Portslade and surrounding areas for our Oxbridge entrance exams. The particulars being the dynamics of social entrance and austerity, vis-à-vis the possibility of joining the European Community under Ted Heath's Conservative government and the projected economic effects upon the working class.' Molly has another laugh and hands out free Cokes.

After a couple of hours we leave. Mickey and Phil head home, leaving me and Johnny to wander down to the harbour. Something about the smell of fish and seaweed always makes me need a slash. As I'm doing so against some building, I look up and catch these seagulls bombing around a little boat out in the bay. Johnny's nervous somehow, not himself. I can tell something's up.

'What is it?' I ask.

'My dad's not well.'

I never know what to say in these circumstances, they always leave me cold. It's like you're supposed to feel something, and I never do. When someone dies all the pretence vomit comes out. It's an act, a ritual people go through. They say stuff that's meaningless because they couldn't care less, not really. Half the time they don't know the stiff. The only thing that's real is the relief it's not them. Mind you, I can't talk. I've never had anyone close die on me.

'What's wrong with him?'

'Cancer.' Johnny's sitting on the harbour wall, swinging his legs, fag dangling from his mouth. The sea's calm, and there are sailing boats moored up. Rich wallah boats, gleaming with money. We don't say anything for a while.

'How is he?'

'Yeah … he's alright. I'm more worried about mum.' Johnny flicks his stub into the sea and gobs at one of the boats nearby. Some old twit with a fake captain's hat comes out.

'Oy, you dirty little tyke, come here and clean that up.' We leg it with the usual expletives and gestures.

Sixteen

I get home about six to find the place locked up. Luckily, I know where the spare key is hidden among the outdoor plants that surround one side of the shop. Mum's left a note to say they're at the hospital. Jamal's broken his arm falling down some concrete steps near the house. I'm about to go back out and head for the hospital when they turn up in the yellow Ford Cortina estate Taras bought on a whim. We'll still be paying the instalments when I get married in ten years' time.

Little Jamal looks more the victim than usual and everyone's faces are down near their knees. Taras turns the *Closed* sign and starts switching on lights and machines. Mum carries Jamal and drags Iman up the stairs. I'm alone with the unmentionable. It's one of those moments when there's no easy escape. Sweat moistens my palms, and I'm twitchy, looking for something to do, say ... praying for *The Enterprise* to beam me up.

'What happened?' I said. I knew I was on dangerous ground asking such a simple, reasonable, rational question but hey, maybe Venus is in the fourth chapter and Mercury might be in the ascendant.

'What? What do you care? Don't pretend you care. Stupid idiot. Clean this place and make the coffee. Stay behind the counter.'

Happy days. In my head I curse him to the deepest parts of hell and beg the universe to let me hurt him slowly, deliciously, painfully, over thousands of years. He stamps off upstairs. I start cleaning the tables, washing up, getting the coffee machine ready. I put some money in the jukebox, play something easy to try and lighten the air.

Iman comes down after a while and says she's hungry. She's so beautiful, a fairy child waiting for her wings. With all the madness in our lives she manages to keep her head high and see the good, see the fun side of life. There's a strength that's amazing for someone who's basically left to her own devices. I don't think Jamal would survive without her. It's sad when kids have to be parents. Although she hasn't lost her innocence, she's got a sharp mind that knows what's happening and keeps well above the murky depths. She tells me what's happened, how Jamal is, and that mum and dad have gone to their bedroom with him. That's how they deal with problems, go to sleep, turn the lights off, close the curtains and sink into oblivion. Hey, whatever gets you through. Looks like I'm on guard duty for the evening.

I make her a burger, and we play table football.

'Naseem ...' She's finished the burger and is having a large dollop of vanilla ice cream with chocolate sauce, eating it remarkably well for a seven-year-old.

'Yeah?'

'Why do you hate daddy?'

I don't know why we open the café so early. People rarely come in till about eight or nine, but it's one of those patterns of behaviour that are beyond questioning. I make a coffee and sit down next to my sister. She's so thin for her age and has shadows under her eyes. It's not because she doesn't eat or sleep well, it's the trauma of our family. I think inside she worries and battles to put up a front of strength. I remember when I was her age how much I wanted a normal family with a bit of love and kindness.

'We're not good friends, Iman. Sometimes, in school perhaps, you might not get on with another kid. You can't get on with everyone,' I say. I know it's piffle but it's all I can muster.

'But he's our daddy! Don't you love him, Naseem?'

I look inside and there's nothing but hate, nothing but the same black bile that I know is in Taras.

'He loves you, Iman. Maybe one day, me and daddy will get along. You mustn't worry about me.'

'But I love you, Naseem.'

Thank God mum comes down just then, looking worse for wear and trying to pretend everything's alright. She's exhausted, and I know I'm no help, know I can't wait to get out. I've been through this nightmare too many times, and there's no answer, no change, no getting better. This is it.

'You can go, Naseem. Thank you,' she says. She makes a tea and lights up a cigarette. 'If I were you, I'd think about your future. You need to sort yourself out. Some little job, anything to keep out of his hair. School's nearly finished, and you have to do something, Naseem. I can't cope with you

73

and him. I need some peace. Iman, go and have a bath and get ready for bed.'

'How's Jamal?' I ask.

'He's sedated, fast asleep. Please do think about what I've just said.'

I kiss my sister and head up to my room.

Seventeen

'Hello?'

'Who's calling, please?' The voice is polite, male and slightly foreign.

'Is Abigail there, please?'

'Who's calling?'

'My name's Naseem.'

'Hold on, please.' After a few seconds I hear her voice.

'Naseem?'

'Hi. I'm not ringing at a bad time, am I?'

'No,' she says, 'it's fine.'

'I was wondering about … er … the other night,' I say.

'Do you … not want to see me?' she asks.

'Yeah, of course I do. I was just making sure you wanted to.' It's Wednesday, and Saturday seems so far away. I had to make sure it wasn't some fantasy. I had to hear her voice. We chat for about ten minutes, which is a record for me on the phone, and, although it's not easy at first, I love it. I love talking to this girl, love that I can, that she doesn't mind, that she wants to. 'So what are you doing now?' I say.

'Practising piano.'

'How often do you practise?'

'Not as much as I should.' We go silent for a while, arrange to meet, she gives me her address.

'I'll see you Saturday, Abigail.' There's a pause, and I'm wondering if everything's okay.

'Okay, Naseem. Bye.'

'Bye.'

Eighteen

'We won, mum … you should have seen it, it was mental. We might have a chance at the county finals. Fancy coming along if we do?' I make two cups of tea and sit by the window in the kitchen.

'Who'll look after the shop, the kids? Your dad?' It's early Thursday morning, and everyone's up but Taras, who's snoring loudly. He suffers from asthma and stops after a few snores, then stops breathing totally and there's nothing for a few seconds after which a huge gasp explodes as he half wakes; the sound of his panic makes me laugh. He does it again and again.

'Can't he get anything for that?' I ask.

'Yes, a pillow held down very hard over his face.' She loves and hates him. How's that possible?

'That's not nice, mum.'

'Who said I was nice?'

She gets the kids ready for school and makes breakfast. Weird how women have accepted their roles in this ugly world of men. When did it start? Why should they be subservient everywhere on the planet? I've always been loved by so many women, aunts, grandmums, and prefer them to the men. Women are straight up mostly. You can chat with them, talk about stuff that matters in a real, honest way. You can have fun, a laugh that isn't mean or nasty, sexual or putting someone down.

Blokes are always looking for an edge, something to have over you. Look at a bloke, and there's a summing up of who, what and why. If you click it's fine. There's nothing like a really close mate that you can trust and get along with, but blokes have this radar of danger that seems to be on all the time, mostly. There's a *do unto others before they do unto you* thing that goes with being male, and it becomes second nature without knowing it. It's not nice.

'Mum?'

'What?'

'I've got a girlfriend.'

'That's nice. What's she like?'

'Lovely.'

'Enjoy it. It won't last.'

'Thanks, mum.'

'Are you going to school today?'

'What do you mean *today*? I go every day.'

'Naseem, you're such a bad liar. Get some breakfast and go to school.'

78

Nineteen

It's so rare I show my boat in school that when I do Easy Easton always looks at me with a cheeky grin, amazed I'm still around.

'Mr Al-Yawer, how nice to see you. You've picked the perfect day. Mock exams next week, so I thought we'd do a bit of research today. As we're approaching the end of term and you've all been doing so well ...' Howls of laughter and roaring that crescendos. 'Quiet please, gentlemen ... I've planned something a little different. Andrew Mackey, draw the blinds, please. Martin Shaw, Samuel Drew, help him.' The class goes into a hush on these occasions, acting miraculously like intelligent kids; amazing but true.

'I've set up the projector with the assistance of our very own technician' (wolf whistles), Peter James, who is ready and eager to get things rolling.' Easy opens a cardboard box full of packets of popcorn and goes around giving them out. 'Now, as you know very well by now, the subject of this term has been *social injustice*, and for your edification and delight, I've chosen an appropriate film for this afternoon's lesson. You'll also be writing an essay about the film, so please don't fall asleep. Lights please, Anthony, thank you and ... Action!'

We watch *Blackboard Jungle,* which is amazingly okay for an old film. The lads add predictable attributions here and there but nothing over the top, and as the film's about juvenile delinquents, a good time is had by all. Mr Easton's choice is a sly way of opening up the discussion afterwards.

'What's the film about?' he asks. The lads are eager for once and give reasonably intelligent answers until the subject of co-operation starts to make some of them uncomfortable.

'They changed too quick, sir,' said Jack Ashton, one of the Ashton twins, who are a bit doolally. Usually, Jack and his twin Joe never say a word. When they do, all eyes turn and wonder who's for the wallop. 'It's tosh, sir.'

'I agree with you, Jack,' said Mr Easton. 'Apart from the ringleaders, the whole class changed from street thugs to polite and friendly prefects, but that's not really what matters. There's an idea behind it that's important.'

'What's that, sir?' Joe said. They tend to do everything together as one person.

'Well, Joe. It's about you.'

Both Joe and Jack say 'Hey?' simultaneously, and some of the other lads dare to titter but quickly gag it.

'Listen,' said Mr Easton, still addressing the twins. 'What do you like doing?' Big silence. Easy holds it, he waits and the tension mounts. Everyone's looking at the twins but making sure they don't make eye contact. Finally, Joe says he likes training his Alsatian dogs, Doughnut and Dollop. A conversation, yes ... they talk about the dogs, about their needs, their grooming, their food and what they're like, and the whole class is totally spellbound.

'What did I just do?' Easton sits in his chair and waits. The Ashtons are looking nervous, wondering if they've been dumped on. 'Come on, what did I do? It's not Chinese Algebra.' The class is silent, not a clue as to what he's asking?

'I listened,' Easton says. 'We listened, all of us, to Joe. Why? Because he was being honest, he was talking from his love of Doughnut and Dollop.' The word 'love' doesn't float around the garbage that's inside most of the lads' brainboxes. There's an uneasiness hearing it used about anything, especially attached to a couple of psychopath brothers who grunt to communicate.

'What's that got to do with social injustice? Everything. Justice ... listen ... justice is about fairness ... which starts with listening. Right, now clear off and come back with a story about the first time you got drunk.'

Laughter, stampede, all back to normal as the lads switch on lemming mode and exit stage left. Easton catches my eye and calls me over.

'Are you going to take the exam?' he asks.

'I'm not sure.'

'Why not?'

'What am I going to do with one O level, sir?'

'That's not the point, Naseem. You never know what life has in store. I'd really like you to take it. I know you'll do well, but listen, it's up to you.'

Twenty

That afternoon there's a bundle in the main playground, and the lads are bees around a honeypot. The excitement of a fight is a trigger that unleashes pent-up testosterone, a rush of gushing, animal, lad spunk. The ones that are not involved are as much a part of the action as the contenders and, more to the point, febrile spectators, who add to the possible enjoyment of the proceedings. Rarely does anything happen of any import other than a moderate squabble that usually degenerates by the time some poor mug of a teacher dares to enter the fray.

Today it's a bit different. Arty Drew is handsome, blond and lithe. He's an athlete, top runner in the Sussex area for his age and the word is he's gay, but nobody's ever said it to his face, until today.

Jimmy James is a one-time hard nut who's gone into decline over the past year and out of fashion. It happens in the line-up. If you don't keep on top of things by constant menace and agro, you quickly slide down the ratings. Jimmy comes from a poor family, like most around here, and is quite thick. He looks like he's an old man, pale-grey skin with blotches and runty, but used to be known as *mad-dog James* in the golden days. Now he's a down and out boxer trying to make a few bob by taking a dive. He doesn't care about getting hurt. Most of the guys get beats from their dads and stepdads far worse than a bundle.

It's rare you see a fight start. Mostly, they come out of something trivial, but being called a queer doesn't usually end up in a scrap. Everyone calls everyone else everything under the grey and threatening skies. Scraps usually happen among the even ratings or if some plum fancies a crack at someone a bit higher. The middle section is where there's a lot of jostling. The top and bottom ranks barely change. This one began with a right mouthing session about naff all. Seems Jimmy saw Arty kissing some geezer down a gay bar and bad-mouthed him over a football tackle in the playground.

'You pigging queer, that was a foul.' They're both on the ground, kicking without any blood to it.

'Get stuffed, James. You're past it, mate. You need to eat some greens, son.' Arty gets up and walks away towards one of the entrances to the corridors.

'At least I'm not a fruit who takes it where the sun don't shine.' Arty takes no notice and keeps walking towards the entrance. He doesn't make it. Jimmy's on his back, and the two of them slam into the reinforced windows. There's a pause as all the lads suss what's kicking off, and then it happens. The merger. It's a spontaneous animal that has a hundred arms and legs and quite a few brainless heads, and they dance, they jiggle and wag and wave like a demonic banshee that's come to life. It's always a good moment to take stock.

Johnny and me look at each other and laugh. Once we'd have been in there with the rest of them, but nowadays it seems so stupid. Since we've been on the scene, it's like the world of school and the real world are drifting islands going in opposite directions. We head out behind the temporary classrooms on the north side and head up over the fields that surround the back of the school, a sort of green buffer before the nearest council estate.

'Who do you think'll win?' I ask without much enthusiasm.

'Arty, of course. He's nifty, fit as a dog and fast. Jimmy's days are long gone.' We light up and sit down on a thrown-out sofa.

'You know there's puke all over this,' Johnny says and looks at me with the fag in his mouth, eyes squinting from the smoke.

'There's more than that, Johnny. I christened it myself last week.'

'Oh, you dirty tyke, why didn't you say?' He gets up and wipes his backside, as if that's going to do something. He starts kicking an old tin can with his skills, keeping it up.

'When you seeing her?'

'Who?'

'Who do you think, the Queen Mother? Abigail.'

'Saturday … daytime.' He starts laughing as he's keeping the can up.

'Nazzy's on a promise, Nazzy's on a date, Nazzy's finger lickin' with chicken on a plate.' I chuck an old cushion at him, and he dodges it.

'Shut up, Johnny.'

85

'We going out Saturday night?' I light up another fag and take a deep toke. 'Come on, Naz, what about tomorrow? Fridays are just as good down JoJo's. I need to move my body, man.' He starts gyrating and back-stepping. Looks well good, amazing, in the middle of nowhere with an old sofa and some boxes. Some weird movie. I start clapping and join in, and we start to sing. Now hold up … when I say *sing* that's not your normal thing of going anywhere with a beginning, middle and end. One of the things about funk is it hits a stream of power, pushes it, twists it, takes you on a trek up and down the valleys of your body and soul. Almost any number on *Funk Power* by The Godfather will blow your mind.

Johnny's punching out track number two of that album, 'Super Bad', and I'm in there with the backbeat, repeating the main line, and we are burning up the dust, man. We are outta sight! What we don't see are some bints from the girls' school who've spotted us. They're coming through the path that leads to the estate and are hiding behind a van parked at the end of the cul-de-sac. We finally clock them and start to get deeper into the funk. There are moments when the dance between the brothers gets into a trance groove. The outside falls away, and you're joined in a way that's hard to explain.

We're clapping and funking and they start to giggle, and we take no notice, just keep jiving. One of them runs over and starts to dance, and Johnny's rubbing up close. The others come over a bit hesitant and watch. They join in the clapping, and I drag one of them into the space and then the other two join in. This goes on, and as it's long past going-home time, lads of all ages from school start turning up, laughing and jeering, but we keep on. Pretty soon there's a mental riot going down, and it's all happening without any leaders. It's outta sight, man. Everyone's singing the tune and having a right laugh. A lot of lads and people from the estate are on the fringes standing there gawking.

Some older lads turn up in a Ford Escort and give us a gander. At first I'm thinking they might want agro. They come out of the car, and I recognise one of them. It's my mate Angelo, the DJ from JoJo's, and he's got his ghetto blaster. Some lads have lit a massive great fire with all the rubbish furniture and the blaster's banging with Maceo and the Macks' 'Cross the Track'. I look over to Johnny, and he's getting well close with one of the girls. Well, this goes on for quite a while and word must have spread. Pretty soon cars start rolling up with older lads and bints, and a wagon circle's forming. Most of the younger ones have all gone home and told their parents.

The sound of Old Bill sirens grinds the magic to a halt, and everyone legs it in different directions.

Twenty-One

On the way home I get off the bus in Hove. Lord knows what I'm doing. Well, actually, I do know. It's one of those moments where you do something without knowing what you're doing but you know you're doing it. I'm going to see Mr Easton. He lives in one of those nice houses that back off the Goldstone Ground. He's not expecting me but seems pleased enough. The front garden is tidy, different from the usual flower beds. There's a sort of oriental feel to it. Loads of space, not many plants, not much of anything. There's what looks like a small tree, delicate, slender, in a circle of fine gravel and bits of strange-looking boulders going around in a spiral.

'Are you lost?' he asks, looking over his glasses with a bemused look on his boat. He must have seen me gawking at his garden and came out. He ushers me in through the hallway that has no coat stand, shoe rack or mirrors. Instead, there are huge, framed posters of black musicians who I later find out are Dizzy Gillespie, John Coltrane and Miles Davis on sky-blue pastel walls.

Choo Choo the chihuahua is in the front room on the sofa next to Mrs Easton, who's reading a magazine that she puts down as we enter. The dog looks up and snarls but doesn't bark.

'Take no notice of the *dirty rat*,' Mr Easton says. 'Sam, this is my brightest pupil, Naseem. Naseem, this is Samantha, my companion in crime.' Most people have all these ice-breaking rituals that don't work. They're so cheesy and embarrassing because they're fake. I'm not sure when I realised this, but it always made me feel sick. At an early age I'd try something different, go for the jugular, see how they take it. Often they're so taken back they like it.

'Hi, Sam. Why'd you have such an ugly dog?' There's a pause where Samantha's not sure whether to laugh or be offended.

'Naseem is going to be a writer who cuts straight to the chase, as you can see. Sit down before I throw you out.' By this time Samantha's laughing, and Mr Easton heads out to get some drinks.

'No small talk, eh, Naseem?' she says and looks at me without a mask. 'I like that. Harry's the same.' I'd never thought of Mr Easton as *Harry*. It seemed odd. 'Have you read any Chandler? You might like his style.'

'One of my favourites,' I say, almost blurting it. 'Did you know he was English? I love every one of his stories, read them again and again. I love his crispness and gutsy dialogue. Mind you, he does walk on dangerous ground sometimes, well, quite a lot really.'

'How do you mean?' Samantha's at least ten years younger than Harry and elegant. Her blonde hair is unusual, out of style, cut like a fashion model of the sixties, a sort of Twiggy look. Her hands, arms and legs are delicate, balletic, yet there's no sense about her of distance. She reminds me of a young boy somehow.

'Oh, you know, there're a lot of poor characters that are black or Hispanic and the women seem to be only two sorts.'

'You're so right. I don't think there's any malice, but it's true, it's no excuse for such a good writer,' she says. 'What sort of things do you write?'

I'm not sure how to answer when Harry appears by the doorway with what looks like orange squash and stands there listening. He starts talking with a cod American accent, as if quoting a piece of Chandler. 'He walked into the room with a glass of ice-cold juice. There was a blonde draped on the sofa with brown eyes, red lips and cheekbones ready to sail into the wide blue yonder. She didn't look thirsty.' He puts the tray with drinks and biscuits on a coffee table and sits next to Samantha with Choo Choo.

'Have you decided yet?' he says.

'Yeah ... I'm taking the exam, that's why I'm here really ... I want your advice. I ... er ... want to be a writer ... I'd er ... like you to help me,' I said. Easton's face lights up a treat, but he plays it down, makes like he knew all along I'd come around.

He sips his drink before giving me the blag. 'Of course I'll help, but you realise it won't be easy. It'll take time, years of study and a lot of heartache and what you might call endless failure, rejections. Have you really got what it takes, Naseem? Writing has to be a love before any other consideration.'

91

'Anything?' Samantha turns and looks at him directly, holds his gaze with a mock look of outrage. 'What about us, Seamus?' I can tell they are performing. It is a good show, and I am jealous. I know there is something here that is fun, intelligent, equal. I have no reason to be jealous, but I am.

'Are you two always like this, or is it just for me?' I ask.

'You see, Sam? Straight to the chase. Mr Naseem ... Samantha, Choo Choo and I are not on the agenda. You are. I propose you come and see me every Sunday at three o'clock for an hour. What do you say? Deal?' He raised his glass of squash and waited, and I raised mine to his and we clinked. Yeah, all three of us clinked.

Twenty-Two

I'm thinking about the English exam as I walk into our café that's no longer a café to see Taras on his back on the floor. He's always changing things, searching for the golden goose. It's a grocer's now. I walk past without batting an eye. He suffers from a bad back now and then. I don't show how funny it is, that would be too real. Taras can't move an inch, he's in agony. I reckon it's God trying to tell him something, but I don't think he'll listen, mate. Me and mum have a quiet laugh upstairs, out of sight.

'Don't,' she says in a hush. 'He mustn't hear us laughing.' Mum's making chicken soup; Jewish penicillin. My mum's a smashing cook. If only she had a nice bloke this family'd be wonderful.

'How long's he been like that?' I ask.

'Since two o'clock. We had to shut the shop early. I couldn't have customers coming in with him on the floor.' She stirs the pot and adds more salt. Our kitchen's the size of a phone box. We've been living in doss houses ever since I can remember. They all have the same dilapidated feel:

shabby, poor, unloved. Mum does her best, but there's no money for a real home. There might be if Taras didn't lose it on the green-baize tables.

She lights up a fag and stands near the open kitchen door that leads out to a tarmacked roof. It's where our poor dog lives.

'Have you got a job yet?'

'Why, do you want some rent?' We natter for a bit. I ask about my siblings.

'Siblings?'

'Don't give me grief, mum. You know every word in the dictionary. I'm only just starting.'

'I'm reading a really good one at the moment by Le Carré.'

'Sounds like French for curry,' I say.

'Talking of which, do you want any soup?'

'Yeah. I'll be down in a bit. Need a bath.'

'I thought there was a bad smell.' I run up the stairs to my room and get some clean clobber. On my way back to the bathroom I shout out to her, making sure Taras will hear.

'Here … what's he going to do if he wants to go?'

'Shut up and have a wash.'

My mum's lovely. I think me and her get on better than she does with the old man. Oops. There's that German geezer with the beard again. Freud. Yeah, I've been delving into that murky psycho stuff. It's so dry, it does my head in. I flick through, trying to find the steamy bits. There aren't any. Siggers reckons blokes are looking for their mum and find partners that remind them of her. Urgh. Dirty git. Anyway, Abigail doesn't look anything like my mum. Me and mum have a connection the old man can't fathom. He looks on when we're jabbering. I can tell he wants to join in but doesn't know how, or maybe he's scared deep down, doesn't want to say something that might make him look soft, sensitive. I think he is somewhere.

It's mental, you can't talk to the people you love because they haven't got the nous or don't want to know. They're fine as they are, fine in their living death. And love? What happened to the love that brought them together? It fizzled out after about six months. That's what I give most blokes. Six months. You hear a lot of old toss on telly, in the newspapers about how love changes, *mellows*. Naff off. Proper toss. That's lingo for *We don't fancy each other anymore but are too frightened to admit it*. There's a song doing the rounds says it all, you must have heard it. Gladys Knight and the Pips, 'Neither One of Us (Wants to Be the First to Say Goodbye)'. So true.

Twenty-Three

At last Saturday comes along and I go and see Abigail. I can't believe how the shakes won't leave me alone; it's as bad as before a rumble. I run up the road that leads to her house, hoping it might help. She lives in this swanky mansion at the top of a hill. It has gardens like a town park. There are high walls and cameras everywhere as well as an outdoor swimming pool and tennis court. I meet her mum who's quite tasty, looks a bit Oriental. She makes lunch that would feed ten people and trundles off.

After lunch we shoot up to Abigail's room and listen to records. Her collection's okay for a normal girl, I suppose, commercial noise, disco-pop. Her room's the size of our first floor, a bit mind-blowing. I feel out of my depth, but she's so easy, like she's known me for years. We talk about this and that and get comfortable on her bed. I tell her about seeing Easy Easton, how I'd like to be a writer. She thinks it's brilliant, says I should carry on studying, maybe go to night school, retake some O levels. Pretty soon I've forgotten about the shakes.

'Don't your mum and dad worry about what we might get up to?' She smiles and puts on 'You Wear It Well' by Rod Stewart.

'They trust me.' She's wearing this quite short skirt, navy blue, a white chemise thingy and looking gorgeous. I'd like to eat her, but I keep it away. Tell you the truth, I can't believe my luck. Abigail's a *nice* girl. The sort you might marry, well, at least go out with for a bit. Thing is, although I'm horny, it doesn't feel right. I'm really enjoying her company, talking to another human being in a straight-up way about how you feel, what you'd like to do. Amazing.

'So what are you going to do, university?'

'I'm not sure.' She lies back and stares at the ceiling. I'm lying next to a beautiful girl, on her bed, in a mansion with no grown-ups about. I try to keep myself from laughing out loud. I make myself breathe deeply, letting go the nerves that are making me edgy. This girl likes me, God knows why. 'Mum and dad don't mind.'

'So?'

'I love drama.'

'What sort of drama?'

'Theatre.'

'Oh, you mean acting.' I told you I've got a duff gene. After a while, a very short while, it's like we've known each other forever. I've never known something so real and feel all bubbly inside. I want this to go well, continue, but as I'm thinking this, a vision of Taras pops up. It brings me back to earth. Maybe that's a good thing.

'What's your old man do?' I ask. We're playing with our hands, tying them together, feeling each other's skin. Hers are lovely, clean and tidy, they look good in mine.

'He buys and sells things.' We start holding hands like we're having an arm wrestle.

'What sort of things?'

'All sorts of things.'

'Yeah, but what?' I start to put a little pressure on her arm.

'He's an art dealer.' She uses her free hand and tries to push me down. I let her win.

'He might not want his daughter seeing someone like me.'

'He doesn't know you, but he will. He's okay really ... a bit overprotective.'

'Overprotective? We could be having it away ... he's let you alone with some lairy kid you've met once at a disco, doesn't sound protective to me. Christ, if you were my daughter, I'd ...'

'What would you do, Daddy Naz?' She laughs at that, and so do I. It is the way she said it, like it was from outer space or something. 'Shall we go somewhere?'

'You worried I might go too far?'

'No, I'm worried I might.'

Twenty-Four

I don't know much about piers, but they strike me as odd somehow. The Victorians loved slapping their metallic inventions anywhere they fancied, whether it was a bridge, a train or an ocean liner the size of a small mountain. I love the old stuff from other eras, but I can never understand the change from one to another. I know it must have happened slowly, or maybe not, maybe it builds up gradually and explodes.

Mr Easton wastes his time trying to explain the cycles of civilisation to us lemmings. He says only two recur endlessly. Boom and bust. The bust comes after calamities and the boom just before. It's not only economic. It's everything. There are bust people and boom people. Bust religion and boom religion. Basically, one is the fear of God and the other is who gives a toss. Bust people tend to be tight and boom ones love a party. He also says it's in everyone. The right side of your bonce is the artistic one, the feminine, and the left side is scientific, the masculine.

I'm leaning over the end of the Palace Pier, looking at the murky water slapping about the girders. Abigail's buying an ice cream and gassing with this old dear who's serving her. The old dear's got about four chins and dressed in cockney garb covered in mother of pearl. Abigail finally wanders over to me with two ninety-nines.

'Who said I fancied one?'

'I heard you in my head,' she said. 'You actually wanted a large one with hundreds and thousands, but there's a limit to childishness.' She snuggles up next to me, and I take the ninety-nine. It's a bit parky today, even though the sun's out.

'Will you go on the rides with me?' I ask. She looks at me, squinting with the sun, and pauses while she eats.

'Maybe. Depends if you're nice. I hardly know you. You might be up to no good, a *wrong'un*.'

'Since when did you turn cockney?'

'Since I bought the ice creams from Doris. Her hubby died in the war, after they got married. They were both eighteen. A few years later she got married to Georgie, a *wrong'un*. He was a mate of Brian, her husband. Georgie was the one that actually told her about Brian's death.'

'Stop, please,' I said.

'There's lots more. It would make a great story. You could write it, an international bestseller, *Brian's Mate* by Naseem Al-Yawer.' As she's taking another lick of her ice cream, I push it into her face and run off. It takes her ages to find me, by which time I've had a couple of fags and wandered into the slot machine arcade.

'Took your time,' I say.

'A beastly boy was horrid to me and I needed to be alone. Are you winning?'

'No chance. These ones are so weighted it's impossible.'

'So why are you playing?'

'To be the exception,' I say, and just then the machine pays out. We look at each other open-mouthed and laugh. Needless to say I put the winnings all back. Tosser.

We do the usual ... nearly puke up trying to eat whelks and winkles. I manage to get a plastic ring from one of those useless grabber machines and we get married and, yes, she comes on the Wurlitzer and squashes tight against me, screaming all through the ride. Then we have a cup of tea and a bun to round things off, and I light up a Winston.

'Have you ever thought of giving up?' Abigail asks. She looks so out of place in this dump, a diamond in a bag of coal. No matter what they do, these places always look naff, so do the people, the cafés, everything. You can't keep slapping on the paint, one day you have to tear it down, start afresh. Trouble is, it would mean gutting the whole pier. Being here with Abigail, I'm filled up with how lucky I am.

'Naseem ...'

'What?'

'I asked you a question, remember?' She tries to make a face, but I stare at her, and she cracks up. 'Well?' She folds her arms and looks away. It's sick. I'm drowning in superbad vomit, man. Give me some more.

'Oh, the cancer sticks ... Do you think I should? Would you like me to?'

'No. It suits you. It will ... kill you ... eventually.'

'Nice.'

She's right, of course. It's part of my make-up and I'd never thought of stopping before I met her. Now there's a part of me that wants to, to please her, to please myself.

I've been wondering for a while if I can do it, I'm so addicted.

'I'll give up.'

'No … I didn't bring it up to …'

'I know,' I say. 'I want to try, see what happens. See how it affects me.'

'You might change.'

'Into what?'

'A *wrong'un*.'

We find somewhere quiet to kiss and hold each other. We smell one another, touch one another, and it's all new, all sparkling.

'What?'

'Nothing.'

'Then why are you laughing?'

'Why are you?'

How is it possible to do all this with someone else, another human being, and they let you, want you to, love you to? No … it doesn't make sense. It's outside the box. We're both out of it, somewhere else.

Twenty-Five

We get back to her place about six and she asks me to stay for tea, meet her folks properly. She's given me a bit of a run down. Her mum, Lilly, is from Vietnam. The other half of her is French. Lilly and Abigail's dad, Samuel, met in a nightclub in Saigon in the sixties. I don't know much about the war and my geography's atrocious. I feel embarrassed about my ignorance. The war belongs to someone else, a real-life American movie. You see all these hippies on the telly protesting about the bombings. I saw a clip recently of naked kids running away from the bombs with American soldiers standing around holding guns and fags in their mouths. It didn't seem real. There's a fuzziness these days with war reporting and films looking the same.

The Arabs I know hate America because of the support they give the Israelis. You'd think Taras was the actual chief of the Syrian army when they get together and start talking it up. It always ends with shouting, bad-mouthing. The hatred of the Jewish people is poison. It seeped into me, like the bullying. Another one of those shameful things you try to

105

forget, try to bury. It doesn't work. One day it came back on me and I realised something. Under the hate there's a coward.

If I'm going to be a writer, don't laugh, I need to look at the other side of the street. It has to be about the truth of things, a balance, a sort of levelling out. In the jungle I've grown up in there are loads of monsters. There's Taras somewhere deep in its black heart, and out from there in circles there are all the others. Nutters at school who are born to be psychos forever. Sadist teachers that hate kids. Adults that put the fear of God into you from the year dot. Then there's the reality of having to actually work to survive. It's mental. You grow up with *The Waltons*, Michael Jackson singing 'ABC' and end up going off the rails, becoming one of the people you hate.

Nobody teaches you the good things. Well, there's Mr Easton, the old biblical voice crying in the wilderness. Thing is, you're surrounded by sharks and have two options, sink or swim. If you sink with all the other twerps you might survive, but something usually dies inside. Swim and perhaps you'll catch a lift on some other shark's back. It feels alright for a while until one day you look in the mirror and don't recognise who's looking back. The coward. I've seen myself being the coward. It's not nice.

I ask her what her surname is; she says not to worry, call them by their first names. It's *Dambois* by the way. Well Frog. When we get there and do the intro, it's all surface cushty. Samuel's this bloke that puts you at ease or tries to. Funny though, it has the opposite effect, makes me nervy. I'm not used to rich wallahs, let alone rich wallahs that are nice. Lilly's just as bad, fussing over me like a long-lost son. I don't know what's going on. I turn to Abigail and she's behind the kitchen counter getting cold drinks. Her mum's sat next to me on this massive great leather sofa. She's getting well close, man.

'Naseem, Abigail says you're a wonderful dancer, is that true?' Lilly's face is shiny, open, there's nothing there of the snide that usually seeps into people. I see where Abigail gets her loveliness. My mouth's open. Abigail comes over, gives me a glass of Coke and wanders off outside.

'Well, no ... no, I ... er ... I do love dancing.'

'So do I,' she said. 'What sort of music do you enjoy dancing to?' So it goes, blah, blah, but nice, genuine. I give her my best *Good boy who won't shag your daughter and run* routine. Samuel steps in, says Lilly was a member of the Vietnamese National Folk Dance Company. We gab for a bit, and I'm wondering where Abigail is and when she's coming to save me. Not that I don't like these folks; they're nice. It's a manky bit weird, man. I'm blown away. They see I'm a bit nervy and leave saying they're off to have a nap before tea. Okey-doky. Don't mind me. I look for Abigail, find her having a swim in the pool. It's mid-April and only now starting to warm up. The bloody pool's heated.

'I've got no shorts.'

'There're some on the lounger.' Sure enough, and they're new.

'How d'you know my size?'

'They're dad's. Come on, it's lovely.' It is. We mess about for an hour and then wander back in to have this amazing grub that's all rice, vegetables and far out. By the time we're finished, I feel I'm one of the family. It's getting late and I don't want to take the mick, so I do the thank-you stuff, say goodbye. Outside in the garden it's lit up all the way down to the front gates, about a hundred yards down the winding path. Abigail walks me down. We snog for a bit and make another date. I don't believe what's going on and she's so easy with it. 'Bye, Naseem.' I start to go and run back, snog her some more. My bus goes in ten minutes, so I leg it.

She laughs as I nearly fall over.

108

Twenty-Six

'He wants you out, Naseem.'

'What's brought this about? I'm hardly here, mum. What's his problem?'

'That's the problem. He's jealous of you. He sees you having fun, enjoying your life, and here he is with me, the kids and the daily grind.' We're picking up the detritus around the house in a mock attempt to clean, tidy. Hopeless. It's an excuse to do something while we gas.

'He doesn't do anything. What daily grind? All he's ever done wherever we go is do the place up and then sit back, watch everyone slave around him.'

'It's no use, Naseem. Nothing's going to change, and it'll be better for you. It's time for you to live your life. Do something with yourself. You've got something ... if only you'd believe in yourself ... get on with doing something.'

'Like what? Make money?' I sit on one of the newly bartered, single sofa chairs made of plastic and puffed to bursting. 'These are alright, mum. Quite comfy. What was the deal? They don't actually go with anything as there's nothing to go with.'

'Shut up, Naseem.' She pauses and her face goes into one of those masks, you know, when someone wants to put something by you they've been thinking about for a while. 'Why don't you try acting? Take some drama lessons.'

'Acting? Think I'd be any good?'

'Give it a go, try something different, for God's sake.' It wasn't something I'd ever considered. I love watching films. I live the actors, live the stories, straight up. I go around for days being whatever I've watched. It makes sense, makes me feel I'm someone. But to actually be an actor? No. That's too far out, man. That's dream stuff that happens to others. I have to say, something rings a bell inside as we're having this natter. I tell mum I'll think about it. She looks at me with that despair in her eyes, and we go silent for a while. She gets back to cleaning like she hates it, like it's sucking her away, fading with every moment.

Being busy in a certain way is a sure sign of some inner insanity. Mum's like a million others. She hates her life but can't get out. She's mum, she's solid, she's all that Jamal and Iman have got. Taras knows that. Knows how to exist as a crawling thing that slithers and sucks up the life juice from anyone that's stupid enough to get caught in his poison. She stops, collapses into one of the new chairs.

'You have no idea what my life is like. The times I've thought of killing myself … the times I've wished I was dead, me and the kids. How lovely that would be, how peaceful, the quiet, the rest.' She holds herself, looks out of the kitchen window. I know I'm responsible for upsetting her on top of everything else, but I love my mum, love her strength, her love of the kids, how she puts up with Taras, somehow

110

even loves him. She's amazing. He's nothing without her. He couldn't wipe his metaphorical backside.

'I can't take it anymore, Naseem. He sees you and it makes him worse than he is.'

'I wish there was something I could do, mum ... wish I could wave a magic wand.' She lights up a fag, and I can see she's near to tears. I give her a hug and feel her tension, feel her fear and pain. 'Listen, I'll leave, right. It's no big deal. I'll stay with Johnny until I sort myself out.' I give her a kiss and head out not knowing where I'm going.

Twenty-Seven

You know Reed Richards, Mr Elastic from the Fantastic Four? That's me, all over the shop with these manky unresolved bits of my life pulling in different directions. I swear I'll end up in the loony bin. Where do I stay? What do I live on? I suppose I could ask Johnny, but I can't see it somehow. There's barely enough room in his gaff for him. I need a job, need money. I'm not keen on the idea of being a kitchen porter but needs must as Taras drives. Sorting things out is not made any easier by what's happening with Abigail. Why would you want to do anything other than be with each other? The next few weeks are some sort of cosmic portal that opens up. We walk through into our own universe. The times when we're not together are the boring bits till we meet up. The greyness, the death of the mundane is ghastly, there's a tugging between two worlds that's exhausting. It makes no sense for normal things to keep going on. What for? Why has it ever come about? It's nonsense.

I have moments when I'm blown away by the reality that nothing matters but the two of us. It's so selfish. It can't last,

I'm not daft, but the brain blanks that out. There's still a remnant of some survival mechanism that wants to be sure of an escape route. It doesn't stand a chance, no place for escape in this thing, whatever it is. It's complete. I do worry about my mental state; I'm starting to sound a bit reasonable. I find I'm swearing less, and even the grammar's coming on a treat.

It's funny what happens when a girl comes along. You start doing things you've never done before. Going to parks and that other strange place ... the countryside. The senses explode, kick into an altered dimension. It must always be here, waiting for the right conditions, only an inch, a blink away. Fall in love, and a parallel shift takes hold, sucks you, whether you like it or not, into the glowing place. What the hell is that? What the hell is the *glowing place*? It's what Coleridge, Wordsworth and Shelley wrote about. All those rich toffs with time on their hands to muck about with far-out ideas and poetry.

It doesn't happen gradually, the glowing. It shoves and screams itself into your stupefied brain, leaving you mental, gagging with eye-popping joy. I sound well sad and I don't give a monkey's. I don't care. There was this thing called *the world*, a nightmare of minefields, war zones no plum knows how to get through, where you can't trust anyone. It's vanished. There was a timeline of dreary days and nights filled with stuff to pass the deathly, monotonous passage of hours and days. There were people who were dead, pretending to be alive, who said things, squawked, did all these stupid things, ate, worked, slept, and they're all gone.

I look at her, and in some mad way I know there are no seams, no distance, no separation. In that place I don't exist, neither does she except as a fragrance, a light that has no shadows. I've never been one to sit still for long, always had to be doing, going, trying. There's a me now that's content all day chewing on a piece of grass, looking at midges going backwards and forwards. My head's empty in a way I've only known with drugs, but there was always a stench in their imbibing, some worldly stain bound up with the ritual. I suppose being in love is an escape, a glorious escape into the superlife. *Superlife.* Shakespeare would have liked that. The old runt made up words for breakfast. *Gloribundus.*

Of course, she still goes to school, ballet, drama classes, and for a while it doesn't matter, the breath of her is with me and she hasn't gone. Well, her body has but not her sparkle, her soul, I suppose. God knows. She's in me, inside me, and I'm not afraid, not worried, not alone. Then I start wanting her, which leads to thinking about her, and it shuts down, the magic slips away and I have to go cold turkey. I get depressed, start seeing the other side, the daily grind, the sad, miserable faces, the old and the dying. I'm back in the made-up stuff, the car fumes and gutters, the dirt and grime. The only thing that helps is to get back to the green, the gardens and the trees. Sad or what?

The home front is tumbling down around my neck, and all I can do is push it away. I try and explain to Abigail without sounding lame; she says to come and stay with her. I look at her to see if she's having a laugh. Straight as a die. Sounds amazing but well weird. I tell her it's crazy, her folks wouldn't have it. I wouldn't have it. She smiles at me.

115

Twenty-Eight

We go to the cinema one Saturday afternoon. I've been going to the cinema since I was seven, mostly on my own. The thing I love about films is, if they're good, they do something, change you, let you dream. The film is out-a-sight, man. It's deep soul outrage, and the funk is laid down by Isaac (The Black Moses) Hayes. The story's pretty average, but that doesn't matter. What's different is the lead actor. A black man who's ultra-cool, funny and straight up. John Shaft is his own man, taking no jive from anyone and not your usual stereotypical *hard man*. He has a right to have a chip on his shoulder, living in a white-man's world with all the racism that entails, but he doesn't. Sounds cheesy, but I love the underdogs. I suppose I see myself as one, being half and half. Not that I've suffered much from racial abuse as I don't have dark skin, but there are other ways.

The film finishes around eight, and we come out into the rain and dark, the lights of the cars, and I'm Shaft with my beautiful woman. It's her and me against the forces of corruption and ugliness. I'm wearing my long camel coat that has a belt you tie together. I've been to the barbers recently, and the hair's looking dynamite. Wide red flares that are skin-tight, fake-gold bracelets and Johnny's necklace. Good thing Abigail's got a brolly. It sort of adds to the mean feel of things.

'You really should come to the drama class,' Abigail says.

'Funny you should say that.'

'Why?'

'That's exactly what my mum wants me to do.'

We go for a pizza to get dry. Abigail doesn't go in for way-out gear. Not that she doesn't have any. Her wardrobe's packed, but she seems to prefer stuff that's, well ... a bit tame, if I'm honest. Don't get me wrong, it's nice but not ultra.

'Well?' she says.

'What?'

'Acting.' Her eyes are sometimes green, sometimes blue, I swear.

'I dunno, guess I'm scared I'll be no good. What did you think of the film?'

'Okay ... bit of a boy's film. Next time we'll see ... *Love Story*.'

'Urgh. It's all soppy ... miserable. She dies, he cries.'

'What if ...' She stops herself. She was going to say something like 'What if it was me?'

'I don't know, Abigail. I don't know anything really. Whenever I think I have a bit of a clue, something comes along and destroys it all.' She looks into me all the time. Never a moment when we seem to be two separate people. Yeah, there's the banter, but she switches to something that has no name in a second, and I know she knows me.

118

Some dodgy-looking blokes come in. There's something about them that's sending out negative vibes.

'We need to go,' I say. She looks at me, gets up, puts her coat on and we walk out.

'What's wrong?' Before I have a chance to speak someone's pulling me by my coat collar. I turn around and there they are. I recognise them now. Wayne and Bernie Martin. These guys are old enemies from the days of the Marquee. The thing most people don't understand is gangs don't forget; it's a code of honour. If you meet someone you've had a bundle with, you'd better be tooled up or leg it. Not possible in this situation, although the idea flashes to do a runner. I get between them and Abigail and stand sideways on.

'Hee, Nazzy, you dark horse ...' That's Bernie, small, fast but full of blag. It's the other one who's a psycho. 'You found a friend to play with at last. We were wondering about you, weren't we, Wayne?'

'Nine-bob note,' Wayne says.

I try the jabber but they're not having it. I walk away ... signal Abigail to run. As they start to come towards me Samuel's car screeches to a halt and everyone stops. Out pops André. I've not had any dealings with him, but I think he's more than a driver. He and Samuel seem to be very close. He sports a tiny goatee and a shiny bald pate. Doesn't look menacing at all; slight, short and wiry. He stands there between me and the boys holding a pair of nunchakus.

'Who the hell are you, mate?' Bernie asks. André doesn't say a word.

'What you got there? You got a present for me?' Wayne says with a gormless grin on his boat. Bernie's stepped back, left it to his brainless brother. I'm standing there not knowing what's going on. Two nasty-sounding cracks and Wayne's taking a holiday on the wet pavement. He's still got the grin on his bloodied face.

'Call him off, Naz! Call him off!' Bernie grabs his brother, bundles him away shouting about *killing me*. André turns and asks if I'm alright then goes over to Abigail, sheltering under a shop awning. He comes back and says, 'Do you need a lift?' Stroll on.

Most of the time we have this pack of cards in our heads – well, I do anyway. They're all hanging about waiting to be used. There's the *Meeting new people* card and the *Oh Christ, someone's died* card and *Woe is me, the world's against me* card. I could go on, but you get the gist. Sometimes they vanish, fall away. For a second, it's like being no one, empty … a nightmare … but … it's so real. It's the joker in the pack.

André reminds me of Bruce Lee. Lee is as close to God as a human being can get. He came out of nowhere a couple of years ago and changed everything. Before Lee, martial arts were for lonely kids and weirdos, like going to Scouts. I'd done a bit of karate and couldn't hack it. It was so square, robotic. There was no flow to it, no dance. Along comes Bruce, and he is the man. He is superlative. This guy stands out from all the others. Why? Why do some geezers have something that everyone recognises? What is it?

For a while, after his films came out, lads up and down the country were scrapping outside cinemas. Nothing much happened, a few black eyes and lots of posing. That's mostly all that stuff is, posing. You look good in a sideways-on kung fu stance, especially with high heels, tight flares and open

120

shirt. Trouble is, it's all pose. You might get a lucky punch or kick in, but unless you know what you're doing it all goes mushy and you end up in a bundle. The lure of Lee was the little man taking on Goliath, taking on loads of geezers, single-handed.

On the streets, there's always some mad psycho, built like a brick shithouse, with about two brain cells to rub together. Then there're the knifers. Blokes that carry blades and use them. What do you do? Stick close to your mates. Trouble is, some of them are up the creek and all. The danger of ending up mashed, cut up, is an ever-present threat you live with. It's part of the game. You almost look for it without knowing. You can go weeks without anything happening, and then you sniff something. An inbuilt warning system. You start to sweat. Your body might shake, and you know. So do your mates. You don't make eye contact, try to keep calm, chat about nothing. It doesn't work. It's like making love. You have to go through a process and finish it. One way or another.

The other thing is honour. Some holy grail thing that Arthur and Launcelot were chasing, being brave, not showing off, not arrogant. Lee had that in spades. If you can't avoid it then yes, defend yourself, even if you get hammered. Movies … they lie, don't they? They lie and we forget the camera, the lights, the script. It's all pretence. Lee isn't pretence. He's the real glitter, the sparkling star stuff that dangles its wide open mouth and wraps itself around your brain when you blink. How do I know that? I don't. Not really. He might be a right wally, but you've got to dream. I'm so glad my street days are a fading memory, but I still love the honour bit.

Twenty-Nine

'You don't want me to write anything?' Easton lights up a small, thin cigar as we sit in the patio watching Choo Choo pestering his mistress. Samantha's about twenty yards away at the end of the garden doing all that stuff with earth, flowers and gunk. Gardening, that's it. She's looking the business, all togged up to get down with it. I'm getting a taste for these others. The ones you pass in the street and wonder about. Well, I do. Getting up close is a dream, a real live book that's tasty, pulling me this way and that.

'The thing is, Naseem, you have to find out what writing is for you. Why do you want to do it and how does it sing in your blood?' He's wearing a straw hat that's a bit frayed, an old grey sweater with holes in the elbows over a check shirt, light khaki shorts and bare feet. He digs his feet into the grass verge and rubs them together. 'I can teach you the basic tricks. They're easy ... you'll get the hang of them in no time, but I can't teach you how to find your voice. I can point you down the road, but you have to wander alone.'

'Voice? How do you mean?' He pours himself more wine and sits back in the lounger.

'My father was a soldier in the Second World War. He saw action in the desert, in Africa, and when he came home he stopped speaking. He did everything he always did before and he wasn't sad or miserable from his experiences. On the contrary, he always seemed a happy man, who smiled at everyone he met. To begin with, people tried to engage with him. It became almost a sort of game. Who was Bill, that's my father, going to speak to first? After a while they stopped. No matter what they said or did, he never uttered a word. Everyone got used to it. The novelty wore off and no one seemed to mind that Bill didn't speak. They realised he wasn't being rude. He continued working as a plumber till he retired, met up with friends regularly to play darts and pool in his local. He loved his wife, my mother, and was a keen gardener. He died a few years ago from cancer, but from the time he came home till he was about to die, he never said a word. As he was breathing his last he motioned to my mother. She put her ear close to his mouth and he whispered something.' He stops there, just as it was getting interesting. I wait for a bit, but he doesn't say anymore, so I ask the obvious question. He takes his time, has a puff of his cigar, waves the smoke away and says, '"Keep the garden tidy, Meg".' I'm thinking there must be more to this, but that's it.

'What's all that got to do with "voice"?' I ask.

'Nothing,' he says, 'but I got your attention and made you wonder. It's not true, by the way, all lies. My father never saw service.' I'm wondering what the point is when Samantha and the runt join us.

'More lemonade, Naseem?' She takes off her gloves and slides her shades from her eyes to her head. It's warm and she's got a men's white shirt on with the sleeves rolled up. Harry's, I presume. Old dungarees that need chucking. Bare, dirty feet. What is it with the bare feet?

'Wouldn't mind a lager.' She ruffles my hair before heading for the kitchen.

'Leave Mr Al-Yawer alone, Sam. He's an innocent.' Sam laughs lightly at that, not nasty. A sort of 'Oh, yeah?' laugh but nice.

'Voice, Naseem, is the flavour of your heart. It's who you are and what you are, and at the moment it's hard to grasp because you're so young, but … I'd say there's potential in your writing that comes from some experiences in your life. I don't wish to pry and you don't have to tell me. The point is, good writing comes from experience, from life, from suffering, from tackling odds and failing and seeing who you are. Not a part of you, the whole of you. All the smelly bits and the shiny wonder. All the grit and gold mixed up and thrown together.' He gets up, grabs the empty wine bottle and trundles into the house. 'Back in a mo.' I'm sitting there squinting from the sun trying to take it all in. Samantha comes out with sandwiches on a tray and a bottle of lager.

'So glad you've decided to do this, Naseem. He really loves your work. He's told me all about your stories, seems to think you have a flair.' She lies back in the lounger, stretches her legs out onto a wooden block. 'Have you got a girlfriend?' My brain's not in gear, I'm trying to string some words together when Easy comes back with another bottle and two glasses.

'She's so nosy, Naseem. Don't tell her anything.' He pours drinks for Sam and himself then goes off to sit on the wooden bench, saying, 'Beware, she's a seductress, a femme fatale, my young friend.'

I watch him and keep shtum, waiting for the next episode of this drama.

'It's true. We're middle-aged swingers who seduce young boys,' she says.

'You're hardly middle-aged. I think you're both magic.'

'Thank you, Naseem. Have some sandwiches.' She gets up and, as she's passing, ruffles my hair again, wanders over to Easy. She sits next to him, puts her arm around him. They both look at me and smile.

Oh dear, oh dear.

Thirty

The next few weeks I do my best to stay off Taras's radar. I'm hardly home. Abigail's spoken to her folks. Not sure what she said, but listen … I'm in the spare room. It was about a week after I mentioned my worsening situation. Lilly and Samuel didn't blink an eye. As far as they're concerned I'm already a sort of Dambois family member. I still walked about zombified for a few days. It didn't last. It's as if I've been here for years. I join in with the cooking, cleaning, gardening and, what's more, I love it. In Taras land I barely did anything. Nothing you do can change a can of garbage. Poor mum did her best, but over the years she'd given up and lost.

I feel guilty, of course. Here I am lording it, having a *Famous Five* adventure while the grime of Taras continues to take everything down the sewers. It's easy to brush off the bad vibes; all I have to do is touch the unchanging sediment of hate. I pretend it doesn't make me a bad person, but I've read enough of the psycho stuff to know there's no free lunch.

Sometime, somehow, I'm going to have to pay.

In the meantime, I'm the new boy of the family. Lilly's teaching me an ancient dance. Supposedly a martial art but I can't see it somehow. It's a series of stances that follow one another at a snail's pace. After a few weeks I get the hang of the movements. There's a flow when everything comes together: the steps, the slowness, the breathing. Abigail's been doing it since she was six. Even though it's a routine it's not rigid. The whole idea of it is to break up barriers and go with it. Yeah, the hippy stuff is hard to escape, man. It's deep in the times which are pretty messed up. Wars all over the shop, terrorists blowing up this, that and their granny, the miners' strike, the end of the *Brighton Belle*. Well, that says it all really.

Abigail's folks may be wealthy, but apart from André, the chauffeur, who keeps to himself and lives in a nice annexe down near the gates, and a part-time gardener, that's it. Everyone does everything, straight up. I'm in there head first. It's not expected, but you can't help but join in. At mealtimes we talk, not rant, not menace, not run a million miles rather than say a word. There's something here that's so rare. I tuck in with a fervour, ask questions, can't get enough. The amazing thing is, they never stop me. Well, sometimes they do, but in a nice way. It's never a *shut-up, you prat,* but rather *let's leave it for now and come back later.* The other eye-popper is how they act together, which I found a bit weird to begin with. They're always there for one another. If someone needs something, they drop what they're doing and step up.

At first I can't make it out. What're they up to? Is it some weird cult thing? Perhaps I've missed something. I keep thinking about that film, *The Stepford Wives.* Thing is, if they are psychos, they're not going to let on. I'm well mystified but find myself slipping in easy. I suppose I can always do a runner … unless they drug me, keep me in the basement.

I went home to say goodbye to mum and the kids, let her know I'm alright and pick up what few things I possess. While I'm there I give Johnny a call. I'm on the first-floor landing, on the blower, asking him about the kitchen job when Taras comes out of the bedroom. He looks at me briefly as if I'm the Black Death and walks by, going downstairs. Our dog, Theba, is howling outside on the patio that's littered with dog muck in various stages of decomposition. It's not the first Theba. This one'll be number three. The first one was put down because it went insane. The second died in my arms after biting me gently to say goodbye. I tried with that one, but I didn't have a clue. It died of abject neglect. The last one's doing well, it's turned savage, left to wander a ten-foot-square area, bound by a ten-foot metal chain.

Animals are like kids, need as much love and attention; none at all sends them into a barbaric decline. How the neighbours haven't informed the council is beyond me. Maybe I should do it. Trouble is, I'm tarred with the same poison. I could have done something. I could have. I blank my mind and get back to Johnny.

'So I start right away?' I whisper, holding in my fear and excitement.

'Come round tomorrow at six and be ready to sweat,' Johnny laughs and says it's a doddle. 'I've got to go, Naz. I'm doing a bit of everything at the moment, so I'll show you the ropes when you get here. It's a laugh, man, some of the bints are well tasty. Abigail better watch out, Naz. I'll see you tomorrow.'

Easy-peasy, man. I'm feeling a bit jittery as I quickly finish packing ... clothes, records, notebooks of things I've written over the past year ... some books I can't live without and other rubbish ... and that's me, that's all I have. I traipse down the stairs. Taras is behind the counter, smoking, and there's a cup of black coffee in front of him, waiting to burn his mouth.

'Don't come back.' It's not a threat, not advice, it's a sort of fact, a *set-in-stone* happening. I don't look at him or say anything. My face is blank, nothing, or as much as I can make it, and I'm out, not worried, not snide; some geezer going from here to there. That's it. It's done. Nearly sixteen years of hate and venom, over in a second. Far-out magic, man. Far-out supersonic.

The world greets me like a wave smashing against the cliffs at Beachy Head. All at once I'm in another dimension and bricking it. Don't know why. I've never seen the place as home and yet it is, in some twisted, sick way that can't be denied. I get a sense of floating and sinking, being queasy, slightly manic. What am I doing? Why's this happening to me? I knew it was coming, was looking forward to it, wanting it. Now it's here I feel I might puke up.

It's a few minutes after ten on a grey Tuesday morning. I'm not parking up at Abigail's when she's not there and walk in with all my worldly. So I head down to Sorrento's, order a coffee, sit by the window. This isn't the first time I've felt this way. I was twelve when the kicking out began. It's part of the Cossack Brotherhood rite of passage mental wallahs

130

inflict on their first-born. Says so in their manual, *The Cossack Mental Manual for Everyday Abuse and Cowardly Bullying Upon Vermin Progeny and Other Chattel*. The motto is tattooed on their foreheads: *Dump on everyone!*

Mum gave me some dosh, bless her, and I haven't been spending, what with staying at Abigail's, so I'm alright for the moment. I'm well pleased I'll be earning soon, though. Money runs out fast, and I've no intention of becoming a full-time scrounger. I light up a fag, hang about feeling sick and try to smile. I'm free.

Thirty-One

Traipsing about for hours with a suitcase … sounds like a blues song. I spend time in the library. Why do librarians always look miserable and wear glasses? She's about thirty, thin as a rake, hair in a tight bun and efficient. Keeps looking at my suitcase, trying to see me stash Gibbon's *Decline and Fall of the Roman Empire*. Every time she ganders, I show her some teeth and a cheesy grin. It doesn't impress. She has a word with a male member of staff who wanders over. He's fat, bald and beady-eyed with a sweaty disposition. Dressed like someone back in 1940-odd. Plaids, starch and polish.

'I'm sorry, young man, but I'm afraid I'm going to have to ask you to leave.' His voice is a bit like a girl's, slightly high-pitched. I almost crack up.

'Why's that, mate?'

'I'm afraid it's regulations. No suitcases in the library.'

'That's a strange rule. Can I see it in writing?' He looks around, uncomfortable, trying to adjust to the situation, maybe get some support from Miss Efficient, but she's being efficient somewhere else.

'Look, I've been polite.'

'You have, mate.'

'So do the right thing and bugger off before I call the police.'

'You'd better call them, John. I'd like to see what they say about your regulations.' He marches off with a red face, puffing like *Steamboat Willie* and talks to Miss Efficient, who's turned up holding about twenty books and looking flustered. They stand there chuntering under their breaths and looking askance. I get up and put *For Whom the Bell Tolls* back with the other cowboy brigade and head off. No need for menace. No need at all. I give them a smile and say *Ta-ra*.

Funny thing about time recently is it seems to be slowing up and speeding down. I'm hanging about waiting for a decent moment to show up at Abigail's. It's only just gone twelve, and she doesn't get home from school till four thirty. Crazy really; her folks wouldn't mind, but I can't hack it. Something to do with pride. Not that I've ever had much of the stuff. I remember when I was about five watching grown-ups performing, putting on their best gas and gaiters, thinking. What's all this about? Why are they pretending to be different to what they usually are? I tried following suit, but it made me ill. It's all part of the same *Big Lie*. Instead of being honest, there are all these initiations, rites of passage that have special rules. Like Christmas and birthdays. After a while everything's some sort of cover-up and no one can remember what's underneath. If anything.

Talking of birthdays … it's mine soon, two months before Johnny's. Sixteen, man. Sixteen. Last couple of times we've gone out together. Not sure what'll happen this year.

Birthdays have never been a big deal in our family. Mum might slip a few quid my way, but that's about it. I can't say I was ever bothered. What's it matter when you were born and why should one day be any different from the next? There's so much nonsense in life people pile up and carry on their backs.

There are a couple of things have been on my back for a while. You might have guessed what one of them is. It feels inevitable ... what'll happen between me and Abigail. And the truth is, I'm a bit scared. Well, actually, quite a lot. Sounds stupid, but I don't know what to do. The funny thing is, Abigail does. She's talked to her mum and dad, discussed it all. Christ, imagine that, me, talking to my old dear and Taras about sex.

The other thing is school, when I bother to go, but I still make sure to sneak in on Easy's lessons. If you're not a wealthy, middle-class snob in some toffee-nosed grammar school, what are you going to do once you leave a dump like mine? Mindless graft that's meaningless, but since you're as thick as two short planks it doesn't matter. Even if you have a spark, the system crushes it out of you.

It's the same all over the planet and far worse: money rules. Money and power, they seem to go together. Easton bangs on about life being in our hands and, much as I love the bloke, he hasn't a clue really. I know that's not fair. I don't know what he's had to go through but can't see him ever having it hard with the readies. He doesn't give up, though. Couple of weeks ago he introduced the lads to George Jackson. He's dead now. American rednecks ended him. It's the same in Blighty with the Paki-bashing, gays, anyone that's different.

I'm not saying I'm a saint, but this last year I seem to have changed in so many ways.

Jackson was a young black kid growing up in America in the 1960s with all the hate around him that's part of some people's make-up. He grew up in a poor neighbourhood and did what he had to do. He got caught for something and it wasn't a surprise. The surprise was how he dealt with it. They locked him up and threw away the key. One year to life. He fought back with education, with intelligence. He got to them in a way that hatred never can. He wrote a book about his life and struggle, *Soledad Brothers*. It blazes, man. It's a star that will never fade.

So anyway, the *levels* are coming up, and, along with everything else that's colliding, I'm doing my best to brush up on the writing skills. It's a breeze, man. Not the skills, I'm not that arrogant, I know it takes years to get anywhere close to average. It's Abigail. She makes everything cushty. Pushes me in a way that I love. We read to one another, discuss the details, the structure, the way different writers see things and lay it down. The other day she read me this poem by a geezer called Larkin. Made me laugh ... *Larkin*.

The poem's all about how your mum and dad can't win because they were done over by their mum and dad and so it goes. I loved it. Loved the truth of it, how it was down to earth, straight-up lingo. No lah-di-dah stuff. Straight-up chunter that said it like it is. Mind you, not all mums and dads are the same. Look at Abigail's. Yeah, dangerous to tar everyone. I'm turning soft. Stroll on, man. Stroll on.

136

Thirty-Two

Abigail's gaff is a mile or so out of town. The bus stops down the bottom of the lane, and I jump off, happy as Larry. Up we go. I take two steps when the limo stops with Abbie rolling down the window. She's back from her school in Saltdean. I timed it perfect.

'I say ... Excuse me,' she says, all posh. 'Are you lawst, only we don't allow riff-raff in our neighbourhood.' André jumps out, takes the suitcase, dumps it in the boot. We sail off to Dambois castle. I'm flummoxed, mumble *thank you*, feel like I'm kitchen staff, and she kisses me.

'Here, easy, tiger,' I say. 'Mr André might take offence.' She laughs and snuggles up.

'By the way, we're off to the ballet tonight.' Somewhere there's this cosmic clown rolling the dice of my days and having a right laugh. I flow with it, man. It's happening and wild and I love it. We chatter about nothing till we're home and André gets the boot open. I'm there with my life in my hands.

'Thanks, André.'

'My pleasure, Naseem.' He looks at me with the enigmatic boat and wanders off. Abigail takes my hand and drags me up to her room and we get close. The thing I've noticed recently is I'm becoming a bit edgy. Perhaps it's the fear that grabs me when there's a chance of us going too far. I tell her I need a shower and swan off to *my room*. She knows but doesn't say anything. It's like she's waiting, being patient. After I shower, we go downstairs, and the folks are making dinner. We help out, sit down to eat. About seven we set off to the Pavilion Theatre and go in. I ask Abigail if there's time for a fag and she says yes if I'm quick and why haven't I given up yet? I nip out sharpish before the curtain goes up on *Giselle*.

I'm sitting on the theatre's marble steps in the warm evening sunlight. In a few weeks my world has changed completely. There's no way of trying to make sense of it all. It's some miracle I have to accept. I chuck the fag end away as Abigail comes down behind me.

'Dirty habit.'

'I suppose you won't give me a snog then?' She jumps on me, wraps her arms around me, plants her tongue in my face then pulls away and runs up the steps.

'Five minutes have been called. I'll race you.'

'Come on, Cinders, shift it.'

The ballet's about a young girl who falls for a disguised lord and dies of a broken heart when she finds she's been bounced by a villain. Not my cup of rosy, but hey, in for a few quid and see what happens. I'm all up for a bit of culture, widens the mind, Easy Easton says. Talking of which, he gave me an exercise for our next meet, and the ballet might do the job. Wants me to describe an event without using adverbs or adjectives. Takes me all day to work out the difference and what they are. I mean, I do use them, obviously, but without knowing what they're called. I find rules so tedious. They give me the shivers.

The very sound of a word of grammar makes me a bit queasy. I think it has to do with not living with it, not knowing it real close like I know the streets. *Adjective,* says Easton, comes from an old word that meant *something added* and *thrown at.* Now if you take a word, say *sky,* and add something to it, throw something at it that describes it, say *blue*, that, my friends, is an adjective.

What the clever bods don't figure is that unless language is warm, hot, tasty, it's as dead as a cod on a hook to most plebs like me. Take the word *verb*, well, there's another plum. It comes from the word for *word*. Now I know a verb is a doing word. So somewhere in the times of old King Arthur, when most people couldn't write for love nor money, the church wallahs who lorded it over the peasants wrote down all these verbs, words. They were verbing all over the shop. They were the doers where words were concerned and so the word *verb* came to be a doing thing. Then if you add something to the verb, you get an *ad-verb*. But what the hell is it? An *adverb* adds something about the verb. The boy ran *swiftly*. Origins. We all need to know our naffing origins.

There's this desk in Abigail's room. It's a straight-up bureau, golden mahogany and built like a brick shithouse. It's the absolute dog's. Samuel had it brought up from the store cellar. Eighteenth century. I'm writing on a piece of history about words while my bint is playing a bit of Brahms. Turn me over, I'm cooked on this side. Anyway, I've got to run. I'm going for the kitchen job. Abigail sees me getting ready with the smart togs and stops playing. I try to explain what's on, and she's giving me the whys and wherefores.

'Yeah, but I can't simply doss here and live off the fat of your dad's manor.' It's not an argument, not a row, more a difference of how we see things about my circumstances. Here, have you noticed how I'm getting into the flow of this writing lark? I actually know a few bricks and mortar of what I'm saying. I love mixing the jam with the Marmite. It might not always be cushty but *Frankly, my dear* …

'Nazzy … do you really think they mind? They love you being here. They're not like …'

'Normal people, yes, I know … and I think they're amazing, but that makes me even more uncomfortable. I have to do something, Abbie. I've lived off my mum and dad all my life … I'm not going to sit around anymore. Johnny says the job's a doddle. I can start today. He said to come round at six.' She's brushing her hair in front of the mirror and looking lovely as ever. I come behind her and give her a hug, smell her, kiss her neck. She turns around and looks at me with that expression that says *are you sure about this*?

'I've just got to do something, Abbie. I can't only take, it doesn't feel right. If it doesn't work out, I'll do a runner. I'm good at that, been running all my life.'

'Will you run from me?'

'Depends how fast you are.'

'Naseem, why do you have an answer for everything?' We kiss and end up on her bed. 'You'd better go. It's half-five.'

Thirty-Three

The job is the pits, the lowest form of life, and when it's busy, it's non-stop. You sweat, look, smell, like a porker. Thank God the galley's tucked away from view. My long curly hair sticks to my bonce after a while, and with the black overall, move over Herman Munster. I've been doing it for a couple of weeks, and the initial excitement of having a job, of earning some wonga, has long since lost its shine. Johnny's moved up the line, a fully fledged waiter no less, making a mint with the tips. I can't stand most of the clientele, rich wallahs that like to show they've got it, loud and lairy.

Out front, everything's some posh film in Paris or Venice with the silver and gold. The tables are tastefully laid out for the clientele and the thugs that dress up trying to look the part. They never do. Muck can't change into diamonds no matter how much dosh you throw at it. There's Greek music playing, thankfully not blaring, and the lights are hidden behind arty décor that talks money. A buzz goes around when it's busy that gives me the jitters, Christ knows why. It seems to move the punters and staff without them knowing.

I suppose it's a bit like the disco scene with the vibes. I hate the punters. Jealous of them. Hate the waiters, apart from Johnny. They all fancy themselves. Hate the management. They ponce about like they're God.

Cowboy swinging half-doors separate punters from the grease and slime of the kitchen. The galley where I live is further still. There are some advantages to being tucked away. The kitchen mob get it in the neck the most. They have this look in their eyes of soldiers going into battle when it starts heaving. Someone always gets slagged off by the chef. I'm quite lucky really; as long as I keep the plates and cutlery moving no one bothers me. Occasionally I break something, and everyone has a good laugh; the head waiter screams, but it's all panto. The boys and girls who serve dump everything into two massive sinks that I sort out then stick everything into huge industrial cleaners. It's hard in the rush, but after a while I get the flow of it. I can also escape into the alley, my back yard, for a fag every now and then. In the quiet times I dream of being famous.

Break times I catch up with Johnny for a few minutes if he's around. We step out in the yard with the rats, no joke. There's a .22 gun for shooting them, but they're too slick, too fast. Poison would do the job, but the owner's a cat lover. Seems the Greeks have a thing for them. We're doing a late shift. Johnny's munching on a sandwich with one hand and holding a bottle of lager in the other.

'So you're staying full time at Abigail's?' Johnny undoes his bow-tie clip, lights up with a fake-gold Zippo, leans back on the grimy wall. He swigs from the bottle and hands it to me. 'Hey, Naz ...'

'What?'

'You done it yet?' He blows a smoke ring and another inside it, avoiding looking at me. I take a swig from the bottle and shake it up. He sees what I'm doing and hides behind the back door. 'Steady on, man. I'm a waiter, yeah. All I'm asking is for a bit of suss, man. No details, yeah. Come on, bro.' He pops his head out and raises his eyebrows *à la* Groucho Marx. I hate the prize rat. I love him and all.

'Johnny, it's …'

'What? Private?' He cracks up. 'Naz, man, it's cool. I hear you, but listen, you need your own place, yeah? Why don't you come in with me, we could find a gaff together?' He gets the .22 gun and flicks it on his right index finger. He's been practising.

'You lonely, Johnny?' I take a swig of lager and hand it back.

'Pig off, fart face. I'm trying to do you a favour. You can't live off your bird's parents, mate. Me and you could find somewhere, you know, a place of our own, man. Split the rent, everything. It'd be amazing. You could bring Abigail round with pride. We'd have a great laugh.' There was something about the way he was laying it down that was almost a plea, a cry for help. I didn't know what to say. We'd spoken about the possibility in the past. I'd given it some thought, but now that Abigail was in my life there wasn't a snowball's chance. I felt crummy inside. Split. I wanted to tell him the truth but didn't know how.

'I'm all over the place at the moment, Johnny. I'm not sure what's happening.'

'Listen, I've got to get back, but think about it.' He stubs his cigarette, ruffles my hair before heading back in. 'You need to wash your hair, Naz. Well greasy, man. Mind you, you are an Arab.' He runs off before I can punch him.

I hear something rustle in the alley, and there's Ratty nibbling something tasty about ten feet away. Looking well fed, size of a small cat. I stand there not moving, and it all fades away. The world and its madness. All I sense is Abigail. No Johnny, no Taras, no mum and the kids. There are moments when I've been alone and wondered what I want. Apart from being one of *The Brady Bunch,* I never knew. Nothing ever sprang. Be nice to know. Be nice to have that place inside. that's easy, sings, slots into place. I brick myself thinking I've got it with Abigail because the minute that thought jumps in, there's the chance, the fear, the sickly dread it might jump out. I grab the .22 and fire. Ratty doddles away laughing, singing *Liar, liar, pants on fire.*

Thirty-Four

I've never spoken this honestly with anyone. Abigail opens me up. How's that possible? I don't know, don't want to know. There are so many parts of us that are hidden. Like mum and dad. I'd love to know who they really are. The secret parts, the private things they share, but then maybe that's bent. Maybe Freud's right and I'm in love with mum and the old man did the right thing by separating me from her when I was five, showing me who's boss. He could have done it without being a prize prat.

The thing about hate is it's a mental teacher. I used to hate who I was because I wanted a nice family, some respect, a bit of love. Hate made me read, run into the other place – the rabbit hole Alice went down searching for answers. I found things none of the other lads my age could give a monkey's about. I'm more mature than that in so many ways, but now and then I slip back into being a right wally. It's something I've not talked to anyone about, not until I met Abigail.

'Who are you, Naseem?' She's straddling me on the sofa in the summer house. The question's trite, hippy fluff, but

145

when she asks it, it's honey. It's the first time it's been asked by anyone.

'I haven't a clue. It's all happening, exploding. Everything that I thought I was before ... that was someone else, someone I hardly remember.' She's wearing a long cotton dress in light blue and white, with a red rose in her hair. It's balmy, early in the merry month. The buzzing things are doing their nut. I push her over, and we're snuggling on the sofa. A sofa mum will never own anything like in her life, in a summer house that probably costs more than a year's café takings. Wake me up. She's reading *Pride and Prejudice* and I'm tucking into *The Pearl* by Steinbeck.

'Abbie?'

'Hm ...'

'Your folks.'

'What about them?' She's twisting her legs all over the shop while she's reading. I'm having a hard time reading that sentence for the twentieth time. I slap her bum gently and she pops up.

'How dare you, sir!'

'Listen, do they know how close we are?'

'Yes, Mr Naseem, my parents know how close we are.'

'But Abbie, we're still kids. I mean, I know we're nearly at the age of consent, but we could have ...' She straddles me again, and we kiss, not manic, not steamy just easy.

'There's something I haven't told you, Naseem. I was going to tell you at some point. It might make a bit more sense of what's happening.'

'You're aliens, I knew it. What do I have to do to be one of you?' She takes no notice of my crass attempts at humour.

146

'You know how you feel different,' she says, 'how you feel older than you are.' She sits back up again, looks at me. 'I'm the same. There's something in my past … It's not something I talk about because, well … it's as if it happened to someone else.' She gets up and starts watering the plants, taking her time. She pours out lemonade from a small fridge, gives me a glass, sits down. 'I was born with a hole in my heart.' She snuggles back next to me. I'm wondering if she's going to say she's dying. It comes in my head. *All over. You knew it was too good to be true.* 'I'm fine now, but I grew up in hospitals, with private nurses, spent years on my own. I did what you did, read books, lived in them.' She lies back in my lap and closes her eyes. I can't reach down to kiss her, it's too awkward. We don't say anything for a while. I'm not sure what to say, feel, so I go for the usual attempt at humour.

'So we're a couple of geeks. Far out, man. Make a good movie.'

'No,' she says. 'I'd have to die for dramatic effect and you'd end up insane with grief.' She's doing all the *La Dame aux Camélias* bit with the cod acting. I jump on top of her, pinning her down.

'But what's that got to do with us having it away? They must know it's a possibility. It's illegal, girl. We're underage, no matter what we might think about being more mature. It doesn't hold water.'

'Who says we're going to do anything?'

'Abigail …'

'Naseem, my mum and dad trust me, they know I wouldn't do anything without their consent.'

'What does that mean exactly?'

'It means they don't mind. Now please, I need to finish the chapter. Mr Darcy has just proposed and Elizabeth Bennet has refused him. It's wonderful.'

'Abbie ...'

'What, Naz, man?'

'You're absolute magic, girl.' I lift her up and we kiss, get randy.

Time stretches into a place where it vanishes, takes longer than usual. I look around for the trapdoor, the one that leads back to my bedroom in Taras land and I wake up. No. It's all real. Go with the flow, man. Go with the flow.

The Pearl is a story about greed, how the idea of wealth can change the nicest people.

'What does your dad really do?' I ask. She stops reading and looks at me.

'Why?'

'All this ...'

'Ask him. He wants to talk to you.' She comes deeper into me, lies on my chest. 'I don't care about money, Nazzy.' The smell of her is lush. I love it, take a deep breath of her head.

'Easy for you to say, you've never been without it. Rich wallahs don't know the half of it.' She doesn't say anything, waits, as if she's weighing something up but leaves it. I wish I hadn't said anything. I still have that plank inside who wants to spoil things. She looks at me and says *I think we should do it, Naseem.*

Thirty-Five

With all that's happening I still manage the Sunday excursions into the whacky world of Harry and Sam. I'm learning so much from the man. British eccentrics have a bang-on flavour that either curdles or creams. I love hanging out to see which way it'll land. One Sunday I arrive to find Easton watching cricket on the telly. Never struck me as a cricket buff ... but he's always surprising. Today he's one of those gormless twits from the Raj with his feet up and a whisky tumbler in his hand. The *rat* is on his lap being fondly stroked.

'Make yourself at home, Naseem. Samantha's drumming up lunch ... don't say you've eaten, she'll cry. Get yourself a drink.'

The kitchen's ... what's the word ... *bijou,* neat, modern. Everything in its place, bright and breezy. Jazzed up with Groucho, Keaton and Chaplin in various guises along the shelves and walls. There's hardly room to swing Choo Choo. I sit on one of the two breakfast stools, say hello to Samantha and ask how Easton's doing.

'Hello, Naseem.' The kitchen smells like a few million others on Sunday. She doesn't pause, busy with it all. 'He's a bit off today, I'm afraid. You might not get much out of him.' She seems a little tense. There's a carelessness about the way she's preparing the food.

'Oh dear. Should I leg it?'

'No, please, it's good you're here. It might take his mind off things.'

'What's wrong with him?' She stops, wipes her hands, has a sip of wine. 'He's a frustrated writer, Naseem. They suffer from cyclical mid-life crisis. Whoever thinks men don't have periods is an idiot.' Looks like she's been crying. Maybe it's the onions. I'm getting the *things aren't so rosy* vibes. Funny how people can switch gear so quickly. For a second it seemed she was someone else, some past version of herself. I'm wondering what to say when she gets me a bottle of lager, sits next to me. 'Have you got someone?' she asks.

'Yeah, yeah I have.' I explain my life in twenty seconds, tell her about my fears with Abigail. She drinks some more wine.

'What you have ... it's first love. It's fragile. You're frightened of hurting her, of not loving her, of losing her. Perhaps you're frightened of being stuck once you've had a bite of the apple.' She'd hit the old nail well and truly. Told me not to worry, not to think about it. Told me to get on with it. 'Come on, time for some nosh.'

I try to eat, but it won't go down. I apologise to Samantha. Easy tucks in with gusto, downs a bottle of lager, jabbers at length about cricket representing the best of a dead, corrupt empire. Explains the difference between a leg spinner that goes *over* a wicket and one that goes *around* it ... stops mid-

150

sentence and heads off to his study. I look at Samantha, not sure what to do, when I hear him calling me.

'Be careful, Naseem.'

I join him in his study. He's sitting in a leather armchair, his feet up on the desk, lighting a cigar. It's a dark room full of books, a large collection of jazz records, various black-and-white photos. It's a writer's room, a hideaway for the artist. It smells of stale smoke and whisky.

'You can write trash and make a living or be miserable for years and penniless. The universities pump out lemmings who know all the rules, all the tricks and are as dead as ancient birds that forgot how to fly. Which do you want, Naseem?' Samantha's right, he's in a bad way. I've never seen him like this. I get the sense he's about to explode.

'I'd like to write something good. I'm not fussed about the money. I mean, it'd be nice to make some, obviously, but I'm a long way from that sort of thing.' He takes a large gulp of whisky from his tumbler, goes to a shelf, gets a small book. It's *Henry Miller on Writing*. He almost throws it at me.

'This man is God. He isn't like God, he isn't a sort of God. He *is* God. If you want to learn anything about great writing, make him your God.' He slumps back in his chair and rambles on about great writing coming from suffering, from experiencing everything, despair, grief and never getting trapped in the mundane. I'm having serious doubts about what today's lesson is, whether I'm wasting my time. Finally he stops, looks at me and says, 'Right. Next week. *Love Story*. Something not quite right about it.'

I leave *The Odd Couple* and travel back to Abigail's on the bus. I'd seen a side of Easton that made him more human

151

somehow. It took him down a peg from the heights. I'm learning all sorts. Around the age of seven my favourite Marvel hero was Daredevil. He's this blind philosopher who lives with a broken heart, but when he swings and struts his stuff, no one comes close. Maybe we live in a world that has to have balance. In which case I'm on shaky ground. I'm having far too much fun, brothers and sisters. Maybe if I don't think about it ... the payback ... it might never happen. Maybe.

Keep on trucking! Hear what I'm saying?

Thirty-Six

When I get back Abigail's waiting for me in her room. We're going out. You know I said she dresses a bit tidy with the fashion – *Girl next door* type of thing. Forget it, man. I'm cosmically blown away. She is something else, not that she isn't anyway, but this is so far out it comes back the other way. The vibrations are scintillating. Dark-red dress that moves with the dance of her body. Her lovely hair's been curled. She rarely wears make-up, doesn't need it, but there's a hint and the lips are shiny. She's laid out all my togs on her bed, tells me not to speak and leaves.

I hear Donny Hathaway floating from downstairs and nearly fall over myself getting dressed. It has to be one of my all-time favourites, 'The Ghetto'. I stumble down in my high heels. Oh my dear Lord ... the dining room's turned into a disco, and she's in the middle of the floor. She's not dancing *Girl next door*. I'm about to get close, but she points me away. Well, my friends, what happens next is ... what did Johnny say ... *private*. Yeah. Let's just say I've never seen her dance like that in JoJo's.

She grabs me, we start dancing close, and I'm thinking maybe this is the time, when she stops and runs away. I give chase, thinking she's heading for the pool, but no … she jumps in the waiting limo, engine running. André opens the door and we blaze, man, we make like thunder, head for town and … stop outside a Chinese restaurant. All this time she hasn't said a word. When I try and say something she puts a finger to my lips. We walk into the gaff, and a beautiful Chinese lady leads us to the basement, a right Aladdin's cave. All lanterns and weird music that doesn't have an end or beginning. Reminds me of some kid trying to learn guitar with wrongly tuned strings.

We settle down in a private cabin. No words. I'm looking at her, still can't believe I'm not dreaming after the months we've been together. She gets this small package out of her handbag, passes it over to my side of the table. I'm gone, man. I'm eating it up and flowing *à la* loon. I open the package. It's a Timex. I take it out to have a look. It has something inscribed on the back. *For Naz on his special day.* I'm floozed, flayed and frazzled. I'm about to gush and then I stop dead. My eyes catch something else in the box. A small square silver packet. Durex. My brain jerks for a second. Only a second. I look up, and there's the fear … so I quickly close the box. Why? There's no one here but us. We're in a private cubicle, it's early evening, no punters down here. Ten minutes ago we were about to rip each other apart. Or at least I thought we were. She breaks the silence.

'What's the matter?' A couple of frown lines have appeared on her lovely forehead.

'Nothing. I'm … surprised. I suppose I shouldn't be. I know we've spoken … wanted to … for a while now.'

'So?' She's hesitant, unsure of herself. Abigail doesn't have street suss, she's an open book. Every time she looks at me it's the first time we've met. She's as new as that ... an alien from a world with no past retention. I've got nothing against aliens, they're the business. Man, I love sci-fi. The other day I went to see *Solaris* ... blown out. It was so ultra-supersonic, far, far out. Well, it was, it was outer space, obviously, but it was more. Mind-bending dimensions, weird in a way I'm well drawn to. Then there's *Silent Running*. Oh, my Lord, Bruce Dern is the nutjob godfather, top-notch psycho. See what my bonce does when I'm bricking it? Runs off to outer space. 'If you'd rather wait ...' she says. She's not looking at me. I can tell she's hurt. I look at her and try to find something, search for words that aren't naff, full of lies.

'Abbie, you and me, we're ... special ...' She looks up at me. 'And ... I want this ... but I don't want to ...' She's welling up. Mad, right? The one thing every lad my age dreams about and it looks like I'm shoving it away. 'I'm scared ... all the hype – films, books – about love, and everyone wants to say those things, mean them ... it's what I want, too, more than anything, but I look around and wonder if it's real. Because ... I don't know a living soul that has it.'

'I'm frightened too.' She looks into me. I can tell she's trying to be brave. 'We can wait.' She wants me to take the lead, it's what blokes are supposed to do. Food comes. She must have pre-ordered, but we don't feel like eating. The owner insists we don't pay, but Abigail won't have it. We leave, not holding hands, and walk out into the grey. It's the middle of May, but winter's not in a rush to move on. There's a bit of a drizzle perfectly reflecting our mood. Funny how that comes together sometimes, almost as if nature knows before you do. It's early, about six by my new watch, a beauty.

'Where shall we go?' I say, trying to lift the mood with a half-hearted smile. André's long gone, so we take a taxi back to her gaff which is empty. Her folks are away for the weekend, they've gone abroad. We walk about the house like strangers, end up in the dining room-cum-disco with the lights still sparkling. No music. The silence is louder than any music.

'What's wrong, Naseem?'

'Nothing.'

Funny how we lie. It's like we can't say the truth because it doesn't translate into words. There's all this mixture inside, a soup, a mess of things tangled and twisted. Some are nice, some are snakes on the head of a Grecian madwoman. They're all fighting to come out of your throat. A right bundle. They shove their way past your lips and before you know it there's vomit on the floor. Best to keep shtum. Only it doesn't work. Maybe that's what Taras feels like when he's pouring out his poisonous pus.

'Come on,' I say. I get up, put a record on, hold out my hand. The smile on her face wipes everything away. We hold each other and move slow. Marvin's singing 'Mercy Mercy Me.' There's nothing can touch that album, *What's Going On*. Me and Johnny bought it together when it came out last year. Marvin was singing about how we've ruined everything on the planet with our greed, stupidity, how hard living is for working-class people. He'd lost Tammi Terrell, his singing partner. Brain cancer. There I go again, thinking about anything to escape from the moment. So I tell my brain to take a leap and face her.

'Abbie, I'm frightened I'll make a balls-up.' She starts to laugh, runs off upstairs, heading for her room.

'Come on, Naz.'

I run after her, she jumps on the bed still laughing.

'Why are you laughing?'

'Balls-up, balls-up.' We tussle. We're kissing. There's a shiver, a shaking between us. She stops, holds me gently. 'What's the worst that can happen? I love you, Naseem.' She hadn't said that before. We both know we're in love, know the insanity of it, but we'd avoided saying it straight, real. It's the *Holy Grail*. Once it's out you cross another one of those lines. Christ, this growing up is so hard. Long story exceedingly short ... we do it.

All those cheap sex novels you read in the playground when you're about eleven or twelve ... the ones where you skip the boring build-up and jump straight into the steamy bits. Lies. All lies. Nobody tells you the truth because no one's honest enough to say it like it is.

Thirty-Seven

'I haven't danced to The Godfather in weeks.'

'Oh no. Perhaps you're ill.' She's stretching in the ballet room, and I'm on the floor with a sketch pad trying to draw her. Oh yes, the bohemian life, my friends, it's the business. Daddy built a ballet room for Abigail when they moved in fifteen years ago. Lilly still goes through her folk dance routines in the mornings as well as the martial art dance. Very lithe, the Dambois family.

'Your folks are well out of it, Abbie. Have you ever wondered what life is like for the rest of us plebs?'

'Are you going to be horrible all day?'

Time has smashed through the drudge *used-to-be* life, turned it into a fairy tale that might do a Rice Krispies at any moment. Snap, crackle and pop. Stands to reason it has to vanish, it's all ... outta sight. Far away there are nebulas, galaxies that swirl, dance to James Brown ... in some underground garden (Easy Easton and 'Kubla Khan,' oh, my word, those idle, romantic toffs). Al Green keeps giving birth to velvet love songs that twist the strands of what's left of broken-hearted lovers' blood pumps, and in the heart of Amazonia something dark and glorious is stirring. It better not be Taras. I get up leaving my stick-figure sketch and start stretching with Freddy Chopin playing.

'What's it called?' She helps me move my legs, turning them gently. Her touch is (sick bit coming) how you'd hold a baby, a small animal, something so delicate and fragile.

'I'm not porcelain, Abbie. You can do it harder, please do it harder.'

'Be quiet and relax into the stretch. The music is called "L'Adieu".'

'Is it significant?' Listen to me, I'm talking ponce. I nearly crack up. She goes over to the record player, gently takes the stylus off the record.

'It's no good pretending, Naseem. You're an intellectual and you love it. I understand why you hide behind the street patter and fear to really dive into what you secretly love, but it doesn't matter. I won't love you any the less.' She's at the counter juicing all kinds of exotic fruit, Lord knows where they come from or where they buy them. She comes over to me, hands me a glass of thick gloop that's magic. When she speaks there's no malice, no telling you off, none of that *holier than thou*. I can't explain. Nothing she says would upset me. It always rings true.

'Abbie … do you know who I am? I'm a street urchin in a seaside town. I've got no brains and no prospects.'

'Why the hell am I with you?' She stretches out on the Afghan rug that looks like it might get up and turn into a mastodon. I snuggle next to her, and we stretch each other's legs in a double V shape. She pushes quite hard.

'I take it back about not being porcelain … easy, girl.'

'*After-stretching* is important. It will hurt less later.'

'You haven't told me about the music.' I lay my head in her lap and close my eyes. I can feel her breath on my face.

'Chopin was a sickly young man who never married – only ever got engaged once in his life. He was in his early twenties in Paris, having left his beloved Poland, feeling homesick. He fell in love with a sixteen-year-old Polish girl, but it never came to anything. He wrote the tune for her.'

'Dirty old perv. When can I see you dance?'

'How about now?' She gets up and goes over to the record collection and chooses one.

'No, dummy. I want to see you on stage, with your school.' Out of a cupboard she pulls colourful silk scarfs, wraps them around herself and starts the record. I'm off with the fairies in an episode of *Star Trek*. You know the one where they're in a fool's paradise? They sniff these exotic flowers that trip them out. The music has a dreamy slant to it. I'd have laughed a crease in the past, and here I am floating off to Samarkand. She tells me later it's the "Polovtsian Dances" from *Prince Igor* by Borodin. Yeah, man, who needs James Brown?

Thirty-Eight

Once you're on the other side of the street, the side where you're no longer a virgin, something happens with your head. It's such a big deal to all the stuff that makes you, a reshuffling goes on. I end up blank a lot of the time. I'm getting deep into all the psycho stuff, reading the underground murk that arranges the upstairs minefield into some sort of order.

Away from Abigail, all I want to do is get back to her. All I want is to touch her, see her, taste her. I'm this raving maniac that can't get enough. The mental thing is, she's the same. There's a look in our eyes, a hunger that doesn't go away and a being together that's even more together than what we were before. We connect invisibly, walk about as one person, know one another without words. Pass the sickbag. No, listen, either it's happening, or I'm losing the plot. The gap between me, her and the rest of the grey stuff is a humungous great canyon. It was already there, but now it's bleak. There's nothing but making love.

It starts out with nothing. We don't know. We know the bodies go together, somehow. We know what goes where, sort of, but as we've never actually done it, it's so astonishing. To be so intimate with someone. To be with someone else who allows you to be so intimate, wants you to be intimate, loves it as much as you do. There's not a clue as to what we're doing, no manual, no advice, no map to follow. We look at each other, and there's a stopping of time. A bubble appears and we step in and vanish. How do you speak, what do you say? *How was it for you?* That's the joke, right? That's all we've got.

Not with Abigail. With her it's all: *What are we doing? What happens if you slow down? What happens if we don't rush? What happens if we stop? Can we stop? What happens if we listen? What happens if we stop, have a cup of tea and come back? What happens if we just cuddle, touch but nothing else? What happens if we go for it, go mad, go wild? How do you feel after every time? What happens if we speak to one another all the time? What happens?*

After the first few times, quite a few actually, of absolute, abysmal failure ... we start to relax, and gradually, the fear lessens. I know by now this girl loves me utterly. She doesn't care. She laughs me out of my concerns. We laugh together, we play, we don't rush, we relax. The fear doesn't go completely. Sometimes a horrible distance comes that I can't fathom. It's the one thing I find hard to explain to Abigail. I reckon it's ancestor stuff. In those days, the tribes needed to have loads of kids to build up the clan, so nature made sure they left each other alone for a while. Seems like sometimes nature switches off the desire button, instantly, a light switch. It's so cold. So empty. I don't know what to do about it. It's like a piece of my love has died. Maybe it has.

164

Abigail listens to me. Says we need to be utterly honest. No matter what. And somehow, because she's far more open than I am, because we talk about everything, we seem to be able to ride the times of distance. Lilly's been speaking to her about all of this since she was tiny and how important it is to not be frightened, ask questions. Far out, man. Like, way far out.

We even read *The Joy of Sex*. What gets me, right, is it's the joy of *Sex*. It's not the joy of *Love*. Nobody talks about that. No way, man, it's all about *Experimentation* and *Mutual Pleasuring*. I'm only a kid, right, I'm only a plum that hasn't a clue, but I can smell blag from a long way off. All these people aren't into love because it doesn't exist for them. They've forgotten what it was like. If they ever had it. Look around, see anyone with ecstatic faces like they have in the *The Joy of Sex*? If they do, it never lasts; a couple of months later they're like complete strangers.

Thirty-Nine

I tried to write a love story for Easton about a young English girl falling for an American GI during World War Two. Couldn't do it. It felt so dead, so boring. Then I thought, What if she kills him? What if they fall in love and things are going great, until the war ends and he doesn't ask her to marry him? Turns out he's already married. He breaks it to her the night before he's going home. It would be easy to make her go mad, lose the plot, but what if she doesn't? This girl's so in love she can't make out what the bloke's saying. It slides off her head as she has a sort of mental lapse. She goes off on one inside herself, becomes really quiet, barely talks, keeps looking at him, smiling. He thinks she understands.

'Did you read the Miller?' Easton asks. We're at the table having Sunday lunch again, only this time it's going down a wallop. Samantha's looking well. Things must be alright, I suppose, as much as anyone's alright. I tell him I read the book in half an hour and think he's amazing – a sort of man who knows everything. I'd like to read some of his fiction. Easton finishes chewing a mouthful of roast chicken, wipes

167

his gob with his napkin and says, '*Tropic of Capricorn*. I've got a copy. The Luddites banned it when it came out in his own country, bloody Philistines.'

'Why?'

'Read it and see. Samantha, my darling, you've surpassed yourself as ever. More wine? Any lager, Naseem?' He's on form today, not drunk, moody or being nasty. 'So what have you done for the homework?' I give him my notebook, the extra one he gave me at school, and wait to be destroyed. Samantha starts clearing the table. I give her a hand. We chunter about this and that. As we're doing the washing-up, I ask her what she does. Turns out she's also a bit of a scribbler. Wrote a novel in her final year of university but never tried to get it published. I ask why. She shrugs, says she didn't think it was good enough. Now she works as a sub-editor for the *Argus*, Brighton's local rag.

'Can I read it?' I ask. She makes the coffee, a dance of cups and saucers. A ritual she obviously enjoys.

'Maybe one day.' There's something about her today that's edgy. Porcelain that might easily break. I don't push it. Instead I ask how Easy's doing. She changes gear, snaps back into jolly mode, says he's fine. 'What about you?' she asks. I'd forgotten her advice the last time we spoke. 'You seem lighter.' Yeah, I'm blushing beef tomatoes, and she gives me a hug. 'Listen to her, Naseem. Never take her for granted.' She's almost in tears. The hug lasts a bit too long. She abruptly goes back to the coffee dance.

'Couldn't he retire?' I ask to change the subject.

'He could ... he's actually thinking about it. He'd lose some of his pension, but he'd still have enough. The only thing is, he's frightened, Naseem. School is all he knows now. What would he do with himself?'

'Take up cricket?' We laugh. Laughter has its moments. Sometimes it hides things, covers them up, makes things bearable. For a while. We take the coffee through to the lounge where Easy's got his glasses on, reading my story. He puts it down and grins to himself.

'You two scheming? Has she seduced you yet, Naseem? Beware of that woman, boy. She'll destroy you.' He lights a cigar and sits back. 'I like it, Naseem. I suggest it needs several revisions, edits, but on the whole I really like the idea. It's not the run-of-the-mill. A simple tale of thwarted passion but real. Well done. Your spelling's atrocious. You really must try harder in that department.'

Samantha asks if she can read it, he chucks it over to her. She apologises, asks for my permission, and I say yes.

I spend another hour with them, we talk about the state of the world, how it's all mad, going to hell in a B-52. Easy gives me my weekly exercise. Wants me to write some love poetry. Oh dear.

Forty

Alright, I'm going to talk about it. Write about it. I'm going to be honest. Why? Because I have to. I've spoken to Abigail, and she says go for it. I don't know if I can do it. Don't know if I've got the mettle, the sparks that come from some other place to light up the dark. I know that sounds daft. My way of writing is to dive in. I can't be doing with the intellectual guff. Guts and heart or nothing at all.

Making love. Making love with Abigail is about growing up, about seeing who I am, wondering about the stars, diving naked into the fire. I don't want to be told the answer. I want to find it. I'm a wanderer. I'm turning into a Class-A plum, – hippy goulash with lentils and marzipan, but I don't care. I'm going to describe it. I'm going to put down what it is, why it's so of the fundament, man. Fundamental. How about that! *Fun* da *Mental.*

I'm going overboard with the reading. I don't sleep. Well, I do, in short bursts. It's like I've got this new, raw energy. A place that was waiting to be opened up inside me. Some extra organ that only starts operating when the vibes are

171

right on. Well, sisters and brothers, the stars are pulsing and it's happening together. It's giving me the jitters. I'm on the beat, man, on the train looking out the window as Kansas glides by, only it's not black and white, it's a technicolor, supercalifragilistic, psychedelic wonderland. Some nights I can't sleep at all, creep about Castle Dambois. There's a spring inside wound tight. I have to get up, go downstairs, pray Lilly's not starkers, or she and Samuel are not getting up close and personal. Luckily, so far, it's all cushty. I walk into the gardens and stargaze.

Okay, here goes. There's an obsession with the physicality of it. At first it's all a glorious mystery and we have not a clue. There's an openness Abigail has that stuns me, makes me more than this naive, sixteen-year-old. To begin with we can't get enough. There's an obsession with the physicality – I've said that already. It's a cosmic flowering that sucks you into a labyrinth of intimacy. A desire to vanish that has no satisfying. We ride the waves of coming together and the love keeps us awake, keeps us invisible, inseparable, whole. And then something happens. The something I spoke about before, the distance that I can't name, can't see, can't understand.

I started reading Henry Miller's *Tropic of Capricorn*. How did they let him onto this planet? Oh, my Lord. He is the boss. Miller writes it like it is, like it happens, searing truth, honesty that shocks the daylights. The trouble with Miller is it's all grime. It's all sordid and exactly what happens when you're a bloke, in your mind, what you do, what you jig about, fantasise. It's the pits, the drain, the gutter of who I am and what I am. But is that all there is? Is the thing we're all dying for, that lustre, that spark that scintillates and never fades, is that all it is? A passing animal urge. I think I'm heading for the nuthouse.

The books and movies, fairy tales ... it's all lies, right? It's the great-great-grandaddy of *The Big Lie*. Something happens when the distance comes that we can't talk about, and, because blokes are so useless at explaining how they feel, no one's the wiser. He wants to love her like no one else has ever loved her, that's how I feel about Abigail. She wants the same. But no matter what anyone does it seems the distance comes between people.

When it happens, the distance ... all the passion, the desire, the love ... the thing that I wish to share with Abigail ... it goes. It's gone. The Frenchies call it *La petite mort*, the little death. They know a thing or two about *l'amour*. That's what it's like, death. Not so little either. More like massive. How do you talk to the one you love and tell her that it's gone? How explain that the actual sensation in your soul, in your heart, in everything ... has gone? I don't love you, I'm dead. I've died. I don't fancy you at this moment in time and feel like I never will, and that's it, we've had it, it's over, we're through. I'm going. I'm sorry. I'm a failure. I'm useless. I'm not up to it ... can't do it. I'm nothing. Worse, I'm somehow, in some deep way, I'm ... ashamed.

I need a rest.

Forty-One

We're in the garden. Weeks have flashed by. It's afternoon and cosy, warm and sharp. There's a spider crawling up a strand of Abigail's long brown hair. It's tiny and really fast. Its little legs are invisible, a blur of cogs that move it along at an amazing pace. Well, it's not amazing to the spider, obviously, but I'm blown away, man. How do they do it? Be so small and do what they do? They have to eat, sleep, mate like the rest of us. Mating seems to be high on the agenda for plants and animals. What else is there?

Her face is peaceful. Her lips and nose and eyes and cheeks and everything … it's all peaceful. She has this light that everyone must be aware of, but for me it hums. It hums and sparkles and it's always there, whatever she's doing. Her dress takes on part of the hum, the lightness, and dances with it. Her dress is a long affair that's quite loose and clings to her when she moves. It's spirals of greens, yellows, reds, and it's humming softly now.

The spider's gone somewhere. It exists somewhere. It has a routine it follows and will go to sleep. (Do spiders go to sleep? They must do.) And where does it live? I reckon they're regular as clockwork. Like the birds around here. I'm getting to know them. You think all birds are wandering about all over the gaff, but no, they seem to stay in the same place some of them. There are some beautiful blue tits around here that chase one another for hours and then stop. Chase and stop. Seems like they're having fun, but again, maybe it's all clockwork.

On Abigail's naked arms are these tiny golden hairs, and I'm looking at them. I'd like to count them, taste them, give them names. She turns on her side and snuggles close to me. The tree I'm leaning on has a girth of about ten feet. It's an English oak, must be at least seventy feet tall. It's so solid, man. It is a heavy mother. It has weathered the storms. It has survived from a tiny sprig to this huge beast that stands there and says, *Yes, I'm here. I am a miracle.*

'Naseem ...'

'What?'

'Why am I so tired?' She looks up at me and we gaze a bit. It's sick. It's vomit stuff that in the past I would have laughed about, made some stupid comment. Her face is mine. It's not, of course. I don't own her. I don't think of her as some possession, and yet this insanity (and it *is* insane, there's no doubt about that, it has to be insane or I'm insane, and I don't want to be insane, but if it means it will go on, then I'm insane, jump in, roll about in insanity and take me to the men in white) ... this insanity is a possession.

'You do too much. Plus we never stop.' I hug her hard and squeeze her ... and she lets me. She lets me and she loves it. I'm not talking sex here. I'm not talking rough-and-ready wife battering. I'm talking our bodies doing what they want to do, and all they want to do is touch one another, and it's reciprocal. It's solid one hundred per cent reciprocal and it's cosmic. It cannot be explained. Oh dear. The old cliché … it can't be explained. Fabuloso, man. Who wants to explain it? Not me.

'Should we stop doing it then?' She sits up and pretends to be all serious. It's the closest she can get to lying. It's so hammed-up it's glorious. She could be one hell of an actress. 'Should we just call it a day?' We snog … okay … we kiss and that's it. There's nothing else. You can't go into that. It's too me and her. It's got nothing to do with you.

Forty-Two

From Abigail's veranda I can see the town below, the country-side to the left and right. The gardens have that hushed feel as it's early and the sun's just coming up over to the left and behind the house. It's my third fag, and I'm wondering if I'll ever be able to give up, I'm so addicted. First thing I do when I wake up is put out a sleepy hand for the Marlboro packet. It's red and white and contains magic juice for the blood of a vampire. It's a box of delights, a mate in all sorts of weather. It gives you cancer and an ashtray for a gob. I think the only way to do it, is total. There's no way I can *cut down*. The venom in the veins is too deeply ingrained. Cold-turkey job.

André's out doing his thing, some sort of kung fu exercise. A strange soul in this whacky wonderland deep in the heart of suburban England. He seems to be a sort of everything man: chauffeur, gofer, security, who knows what else. I'm not keen on the idea of his always being in the background whenever me and Abigail go anywhere, but it's part of the deal apparently. So far, I've never seen him, apart from the incident after the cinema. He keeps to himself, but I catch him giving me the once-over every now and then. I smile and he smiles back, but that's as far as I get. I'm not pushing it. There's something good about him, invisible. It's as if he's not there and yet he is. Well weird.

The rich are so clever with their hideaways. You think they're mostly safe in hotspots in the south of France, Biarritz, but they're everywhere, tucked away, invisible. I'd like to know what Samuel does and whether I can cut a piece of the cake, a smidgen, a tiny smidge off the icing. Not that I've ever given a toss for money. I've seen what it does to people, makes them ugly mostly, changes them beyond recognition.

Abigail comes up behind me, puts her arms underneath mine, holds me, and I'm a king. I'm a Cheshire smiler with not a care and take it while I can. That sounds mercenary. Not what I mean. I'm frightened. Recently the old chestnut keeps popping in the box that I'm not good enough, that it won't last, can't. I push it away, keep running towards her. She saves me with her love. It has no end, no shadows.

'Why are you up?' Her voice is drowsy, slurry, delicious.

'I'm being Ernest Hemingway in Mexico.'

'What did he do there?'

'He went to the races.'

'What's it like?'

'What?'

'Being Hemingway?'

'I drink too much, don't wash enough, I'm hairy and my chest is too big.' I turn around and smell her. Smell her sleepy eyes and mouth that have all the night's adventures, tastes. 'You talk in your sleep.'

180

'I don't.'

'Yeah, you kept saying Naseem, I love you, Naseem, I love you.'

'Why would I say such a silly thing?' She pulls down the pyjama bottoms I'm wearing and runs back into the room. Oh dear. It's all sick. Glorious, technicolor vomit. Love it.

Forty-Three

I still do other stuff. See Easton and Sam. Go to work. Johnny's been banging on about our birthday bash. I promised him I would, even though my heart's not in it. I feel a right prat about it all. Since Abigail, I've not gone out once. All that stuff belonged to someone else. Being in love has giving me new insights into who I am. Some parts are not nice. I talk to her about it, she gets straight to the point.

'Be honest with him. He's your best friend ... he must feel hurt. I know I would. I feel responsible for taking you from him. You should see him, Naseem.' Sounds easy, but I know it won't be. Next time I see him at work we make a date. The day arrives, and I go round to his place with a present. He opens the door and stands there with the grin.

'Who are you, mate?'

'Shut up, Johnny. Here, guess what it is.' He laughs at the wrapped-up album I bought him, and we scoot up to his room. He jumps on his bed, throws me what looks like a book. Usual thanking chunter and that. I open it up, and it is a book. One I've wanted for a while, *The Outsider* by Colin

Wilson. I'm amazed Johnny even knows about my interests, ask how he decided to get it.

'I didn't, Naz. Easy Easton helped me out. Happy birthday, sunshine.'

'Thanks, Johnny.' He starts unwrapping the album.

'She's a good wrapper,' he says and smiles without looking up.

'Yeah, alright, Johnny, lay off with the sarky.'

'My word, Naz, *These Are the JB's*. This must have cost a mint! It's an import, brother. I can't take this, man.'

'Stick it on, Johnny.' He does, and we finish off adding the last touches to the body beautiful. We talk about the old days, the scrapes we've been through, the fights, the bints we nearly landed but never did. The sounds, the lads that introduced the scene and wonder how they're doing. After a while we're quiet and I know what's coming. Johnny takes the record off.

'Thanks for this, Naz.'

'Happy birthday, mate.'

'How's it going with Abigail?' He's polishing his platforms and looks up at me, waiting.

'It's amazing, Johnny.' I'm hoping he doesn't ask the obvious question. The one that we've waited so long to answer.

'You've had it, mate.' Johnny's combing his locks like he's being filmed. His hair's quite wispy as it happens. *Widow's peak* they call it. I don't say anything serious, make a joke he's going bald, and he knuckles me.

'What d'you mean?' I know exactly what he means, but I'm trying to play it cool, change the subject, rummage through his records. 'Here, you've been busy,' I say. 'I've got this one. You could have borrowed it.' He doesn't take the bait, pushes me out the way and gets his jacket from the wardrobe. 'Look,' I try, 'I know things have changed, but …' He goes over to his record player, takes the record off.

'You're in love, Naz. That's bad, man. You've broken the first rule of the brothers. Never get serious.'

Sometimes I hate life. You try to be everything to everyone and you can't be. There are traps set by some unknown alien from the Beta Quadrant to see what you're made of. You can blag it for a while, make out you're in charge, know what you're doing. It doesn't cut it. Whatever it is hits you with a knockout punch and you're down and out. That's what happens when things change. It might be something you've been dreaming about, but when it comes you're not so sure about anything. You lose a part of yourself, a part that's so familiar it leaves you wondering, Who the hell am I? What's going on? What do I do? You pretend nothing's changed, but it doesn't work. There's a tug of war going on between the old and the new. You know who's going to win, but you're on shaky ground, haven't quite crossed over, feel sick, feverish, like you're coming apart. I leaf through a copy of *NME* that's on the floor.

'Where are we going?' I ask.

'Why don't we try somewhere different?' He grabs the mag and jumps on the bed.

I can tell there's something up. Johnny's a man who doesn't like change. He's wearing his best tonight, black-satin loons, white T-shirt and black, crushed-velvet jacket. Now he's earning good dosh he's looking the business. He jumps up, whacks me on the head with the mag. 'Come on, man. Let's go.' It feels so strange to be back with Johnny, doing the old stuff. It's as if I'm slipping out of one skin into another. I find my old ways of thinking, speaking, even the way I sit in my body, coming back no trouble. Psycho, man. Superpsycho.

We stop by an offy, and Johnny goes in to get fags. I kid myself I never wanted to start smoking, that I did it to spite Taras, not that I would've ever dared to tell him. He smokes twenty a day, but there's another of those unwritten laws that I must never, ever smoke. Hypocrite. That word cuts like a knife. Slides off the tongue in a delicious way. Yeah, I'm getting well into the lingo. Don't think I'll ever write as good as the greats. You never know, I might give Taras a heart attack, go to university. Fat chance. Thickos like me don't go that way, we live in the grime and blood of the streets. The sweet wallahs that run this world have it all shorn up nicely.

Johnny comes out the offy and chucks me a packet of Marlboros. I take one from an open packet he's offering and light up. There's a whole language to smoking, a dance to it. I suppose everyone who smokes knows about it and perhaps even those that don't. At first it makes you sick, your mates laugh, whack you on the back, say things like 'Don't worry, you plank, you'll get used to it.' Why? Why get used to the most horrible taste, inhale all that tar, poison, into your flesh and blood that gives you cancer? It's one of those lies. There are so many of them it's hard to keep up. The lie that people love one another, love their kids, love their family, mates, pets. It's a load of tosh. Most people put up with being dead. Their lives are horrible, full of pain, but they go about saying *Mustn't grumble* or *Could be worse*.

It's not only the way you smoke. It's a whole way of life that has different compartments. There's what you smoke, how you light up, what with, how you draw the smoke and let it out. It's how you fidget with the fag, play with the box, whether you chain-smoke or only now and then. Then there's the deeper. All cults have a deeper. Smoking's a stupid cult that makes faceless idiots millions from the addictive properties of nicotine and the social poncing people do with a cancer stick stuck in their mouths or between their fingers. The deeper with smoking is posing. The way you light up with your mates, hunched over, cupping your hands. There's not a whisper of a wind anywhere, but it looks good. It's the way you blow smoke rings, experiment with different brands. Anyone who's cool smokes Marlboro, and the coolest of the lot is Winston, but they're hard to find. Arty-farties smoke that French muck, Gitanes, and real nutters smoke Camel or Lark. A couple of those and I feel sick, have to lie down. I smoke because I'm an idiot who doesn't know better. I smoke because I think it's cool like all the other wallys. I smoke because I'm addicted and don't realise it or won't even contemplate looking at it. I smoke because I'm a working-class teenager.

I think they're coming to an end ... my smoking days.

Forty-Four

Wherever you go at night in this town you need to have your wits about you. It seems trouble never touches some people and always gets others. Johnny's heading for the Seven Stars, a right old dump that's been tarted up fresh under new management. It has this reputation. Basically, nutjobs go there to get stuck in. All that's long behind me. If it wasn't for Johnny, I'd never set foot in the place. See what love does? I look at other birds and see Abigail, it's well weird. I've lost the stare. I used to be bad that way when I cottoned on to the scene, desperately trying to lose the cherry with *gay abandon*.

I love that phrase. Mr Manton, our French teacher, uses it like a lord. I feel so sorry for him; he's another old stiff but harmless. The lads always give him gyp. Most teachers at my school are throwbacks from World War Two. They all needed to die along with that fiasco. Anyway, Manton's about seven-foot tall and his wifey's about three. No word of pork. He tries hard to instil a love of the Frog, but it falls on *les oreilles sourdes*. I do like French. It's got a lightness that takes my fancy. Abigail's a master; wants us to go to Paris. Who knows? Nothing surprises me these days.

Even though Johnny and me haven't been out for a while it doesn't take long to get back in the flow. I'm feeling a bit jittery but settle down after a few mouthfuls of lager. In the Stars, there's a raised platform for dancing, and around the outside all the brothers swagger and pose. Then there's the bar lot that gas all the time. We find a dark corner that commands a good view, wait for the right sounds.

This night the menace isn't there. It's calm, people are enjoying themselves. Most of the clientele are posh wallahs that rabbit ten to the dozen, throw back their heads, laugh every now and then. Funny how you never know many people. I mean, I know Abigail, Johnny, a few Arabs, and that's it. Then there're all these clowns that are faceless. You might recognise a nutjob to keep out of his way, but all the others are ghosts.

The main thing is the dancefloor which is small in the Stars but enough. Out of the two of us, I'm usually the first on. I love it, love being in the heart of it. Takes guts to get out there on your tod, you better be good or your mates will laugh. William DeVaughn comes on with 'Be Thankful for What You Got', and I'm on. There's a rush that everyone who dances takes for granted. You see it in a crowd that's bouncing along, and then a special sound comes on that changes the atmosphere. I love it and hate it. Reminds me of a herd of animals.

Johnny's quite shy under the pose. He comes on next to me, and after a bit we're burning like the old days. This loaded bint comes on, starts to dance in front of him, and I suss the reason we're here. This must be the new girlfriend. Thing is, something's not quite right with what's going down. She's way out of his league, it doesn't feel right, so I exit the song halfway and put the agro radar on top alarm. Johnny looks over to where I'm sitting on a metal sidebar that goes around the dancefloor. He smiles like everything's okay and doing his thing when it all goes belly up. I knew it, clobbering time. Leather boys, well, men ... no boys here.

When something happens too fast it means you've been lazy. If some nutter wants a fight you know about it well in advance and steer clear. Always avoid trouble if you can. It comes with experience, and after a few battles you get the message. When it catches you out it's only later you can look back and see the signs.

A haze comes in these situations that must be animal. For a tiny moment the internal mechanism kicks in, all that *fight or flight* tosh. A part of you splits into this plum that wants to run, and you move, your body moves to leg it. Then another part jumps out and says, *Nah, get lost, I'm in there to help my mates.* That's when it's beautiful, the courage, the insanity, the stepping into another dimension where time, what's right and wrong, have vanished. You might get pummelled, kicked to blackout or worse. You're not thinking about that, not thinking at all, it has no place in this moment. Here, don't get me wrong, I'm not condoning it, I'm telling you what happens. Well, to me anyway.

There's glass being smashed somewhere. All sorts of stuff happening. One on one. Two on one. There's some on the floor, some standing. Mayhem. Somehow, I manage to get a couple of leather boys away from me and jump up on the metal sidebar. I see Johnny getting a kicking. I'm over there

191

and grab him away. By that time the bouncers are doing their business. They always come late when it's more than one or two. Crafty.

We leg it through the ghost punters who look on incredulously, affably, indifferently, and out into the evening summer beams where everything's cosy. Johnny's head is gashed a bit and my lip's bleeding but nothing much. There's a public toilet around the corner known for dirty old men. We bundle in and, sure enough, in the corner there's an old git wearing a dirty mac, pretending to have a slash. He's got a fiver in his mouth and looks at us with a worried look on his boat. We laugh as we wash our cuts in the filthy basins.

'Why didn't you warn me?' We've got over the adrenalin rush, walking along the prom. It's gorgeous with blood-red on the horizon. Here and there pinky clouds are hanging about, waiting for something, a breeze maybe. I sit down on a bench that has vomit on one side caking up. The council are useless. The place could do with a bit of money splashed on it, but there's never much left for the common man. Rich wallahs don't give it away. Johnny looks a bit sad. I suppose he's feeling guilty, which he should, but I love him, so I go easy.

'Who is she?'

'Penny Devonshire, Charlie's daughter.' Charlie Devonshire's one of the big boys in this town. Quite close to the top dogs and known for being violent. He owns streets of houses, and there's talk he's moving into casinos. I know this from some of my Arab mates who like to frequent them. He has gangs of leather boys do his dirty work, psychopaths that'll give you a nice hospital holiday for the right money.

'So what's the game? You know he won't let her go with just anyone. She's out of your league, mate.'

'You can talk, you ain't been around for months. I got bored of Sandra. Penny came up to me a few weeks ago in the Stars ... we started chatting.'

'What about ... football?' I'm being a right prat because I can see his point. Even as we're talking, after being in a rumble and getting out okay, it all feels odd. It's not the same. I've changed. I haven't been on the scene for months. Time and distance have come between us. We walk down to the edge of the shore. 'So what are you going to do?' I ask. He looks down at his shoes, natty black platforms with a brogue front, and kicks at the pebbles.

'I'm not giving her up. I don't know, see what happens.'

'I know what'll happen. You'll end up with a new face.'

He looks at me and slowly starts to smile. I love his smile, it always makes me laugh. We start play-fighting, rumble around on the beach. It's getting dark, we should be getting home but we're in this limbo-land, don't really know what to do. It's like we know something might be ending.

'Here, why don't we jack a car?' Johnny lays back with his hands under his head.

'Are you mad? We can't drive.'

'I can. Ricky Berring gave us a go up near the rec the other day. He's got this old banger, drives around like a boss.'

Ricky is top-notch hard, or at least he was until he got into the weed. Most of the local nutters have no heart; they'll kick your head in for a laugh and not think twice. Ricky's different. He comes from an ordinary family who live on the estate with about fourteen brothers and sisters, an old

193

man who's a lush, an old dear who's dying from being a skivvy. Ricky and thousands of others should have been sent to the army at the age of thirteen. That's my answer to the hooligan problem. None of these lads could give an eggy fart about geography or 1066. As for the other subjects, physics, chemistry, art, give it a right royal rest; you might as well teach ants to sing the national anthem.

Trouble is there's nothing out there once you leave school unless you want to brown-nose and get paid a pittance. So what can they do? Most of the lads can't tie their shoelaces. Crime's the easy answer. It's an old story. Ricky's turned dealer. Old Bill know he's in the game and give him a bit of leeway to suss the big boys. They never do. The big boys own the Bill, the courts and the briefs.

The rec, or recreation ground, is a piece of land behind the housing estate where Johnny lives. Kids get up to mischief there, grope one another, get drunk and imbibe dangerous sweeties. I've never touched the place. It's like a dead land that zombies inhabit when it's full moon. Someone always ends up mangled, or worse.

'What the hell were you doing up the rec with that twazock?'

'He's alright, as it happens. Mind you, he is into 10cc.' Johnny cracks up with that and belly laughs. You know sometimes you get a laugh you can't shake off? It takes you over, and after a while you don't know what you're laughing for. The thing that made you laugh isn't even that funny, it's the laughing itself. You turn into a right lemon who can't stop and nearly die with it. Trouble is, it's catching. I look at him, and he's gone, and then I start. This goes on for some

194

time. Finally, we lie there in the dark, exhausted. The stars are out and it's starting to get a bit nippish.

'Listen,' I say, 'I know we haven't …' But Johnny gets up and starts to walk away.

'Not going soft, are you, Naz? Next thing you'll be getting married, or worse.'

'What's worse than getting married?'

'I don't know,' he says. 'Maybe thinking something'll last forever when nothing ever does?'

He's trying to say something about our friendship in a roundabout way, and I feel myself getting angry.

'What are you talking about?'

'You're starting to be normal, man. You're starting to forget the scene, the sounds, the soul. You know you'll get fed up after a while. It's not like you've said anything about her, so it must be serious.'

We're having a row. Me and Johnny are actually having a row. He's right, of course. I probably will get fed up with Abigail. I can't see how I won't. You look around at anyone you know that's been together a few months, and it's dead, or they're lying, pretending. People get sick of each other, bored. It's only natural. If you eat too much of one thing it gets samey, bland. I'm talking out of my nether regions here as I don't know, not from experience. What's happening with Abigail is still fresh, still baking, and take a gander at my heart floating somewhere in outer space. I want to share it with Johnny, tell him how I feel, want him to be part of it. Nutter.

We reach a point where we stop walking, talking. It's hard now. I don't know what to say. Johnny looks at me.

'It's alright, Naz. We'll always be mates, no matter what happens.' I'm welling up, and he walks off.

After a while I shout after him, 'I'll give you a ring.' Johnny waves his hand without turning around as if to say, *Yeah, we'll see.*

Forty-Five

I creep back around three in the morning and have a stroll in the garden for a bit. The early hours are magical, a tacky horror film, with all the different sounds, smells, lights that we miss. There's a fear grabs you when you're alone in the shades. Stupid. Take the garden. How different is it from the day, apart from the light? Yeah, there's another shift on. A new set of little night creatures enjoying the flavour, but apart from that, what? Monsters, demons, ghosts? Why do those wallahs only roam in the gloom? How many people have actually seen anything and can you believe them? The numbers are tiny, and you can never be sure. Don't get me wrong, I'd love to know there's something other than this merry dance, but unless you bump into grandma and have a chinwag, all you've got is noise. Someone else's say-so. The chances of being jumped on by the dead seem to be quite slim, but we still brick ourselves. Why is that?

Abigail's asleep. I sit on a sofa and let it all go. All the noise and jive of family, friends, things I think I can and can't control. It's all tosh. Half the time we don't have a clue and the other half's a mystery. I've had these weird dreams now and then, felt I was travelling to some place before we came to this nightmare. A quiet, happy hunting ground with all the fairies and that, only they're not what we think they are. When I wake up I still have the smell of the place, a shadow that danced out of the corner. It tingled inside, made me smile the way a baby smiles at its mum. Trouble with dreams is they always end.

Why am I having a mare? Because I love my mate, know he needs me but I can't do it. I can't split myself for him. I can't lose a minute of Abigail. I know if I do it'll be the beginning of the end. I haven't got whatever it is to be there for him. It's one or the other. Nothing's easy in this movie. It's a cheap budget fix-up that never made it past the cutting desk. Somewhere my brother and sister are sleeping. Somewhere there's a place where they're loved, have fun, are cuddled, played with, given time, made to feel safe. It's not this sorry parade. Here, the monsters and ghouls are real. They're me and you. So belt up and take the ride.

It's not like I'm not having a laugh. I'm drowning in the glowing. I'm head over heels with a fairy-tale princess in her fairy-tale castle. On the surface I'm giving it easy, going with the flow, but nothing's what it seems. There's an underbelly that lurks. It's soft, fat, full of poison. Still, you never know. So far my luck's been top-notch. I've deserted my mum, my siblings, my best mate, and I'm rolling about in clover. Don't know who's holding the cards, but mine are aces high. I know there'll be a reckoning. No point stressing.

I get undressed, try to be quiet getting into bed, but Abigail wakes up and gets close. She's blurry, smells nice. I kiss her face.

198

'Don't wake up. It's early.' She turns around and I cuddle into her.

'How did it go?'

'Okay.'

'You're lying … you've got a cut lip. What happened?'

'I'll tell you tomorrow. Go to sleep.' She's gone before I finish the sentence. The honest truth is, she snores. Not loud, not flapping wings … a sweet, soft, gentle snore that's lovely. It helps me trundle into dreamland where strange animals fight in the dark, change into little children playing hide and seek … Johnny's there on a sofa, out of his head, smoking a hubbly bubbly. He's quoting a bit of 'Kubla':

Weave a circle round him thrice,
And close your eyes with holy dread,
For he on honey-dew hath fed,
And drunk the milk of Paradise.

Easy Easton comes in dressed as the Sheik of Araby on a little train pulling Samantha, who's wearing skimpy leathers, high heels and cracking the whip. Dreams … it's a good thing we forget most of them.

Forty-Six

Next morning I wake to someone breaking down the door with a sledgehammer ... in my head. Abigail's singing. She's having a bath. I get up all groggy, fall into the en suite and land on the khazi.

'Are you having an affair, Naseem?'

'Yeah, with a rhino.'

'Why don't you come in. Looks like you need it.' She washes my back as I sit there in front of her almost nodding off.

'How did it go?' I give her a rundown, keep out the gory bits, try to explain how I feel about Johnny, and she listens. I'm not really up to it, keep it short. She knows I'm not opening up but doesn't push it. Instead, she gets out, dries off and leaves me to soak. I mumble that I love her.

Half an hour later I drag myself out. She's made breakfast that's laid out on the balcony. It's nine thirty and the sun's streaming in. I'm there with nothing but the towel. She's in a sunhat, dark shades, elegant dress and blouse.

'You being mother?' She takes no notice as I sit there and take stock of my empire. We gas about nothing. Then she talks about how we need to not take each other for granted. I'm tucking into croissants, jam, honey, coffee that smells of rich soil and she's making me cry.

'We have to find a way not to die, Naseem.'

'What are you talking about? Are we dying?'

'Not yet.' Being someone who's had to live with the possibility of death has made this girl so up front. She astounds me. I keep looking to see if she's going to vanish.

'How do we not die? What do you mean exactly?' She tells me she can't explain in a rational way, but her feelings tell her, her intuition, that we have to be different. I ask her to be more specific.

'There's a danger the lovemaking will become habitual.' Whoa … there it is. Not tucked away, not hinted at or alluded to. Bang. Thing is, it's how we've been since the start. We talk about it. Well, she talks, I open up and follow. It's a dream place that's more real than anything this sham world has going for it.

'What should we do?'

'I'm not sure.' She pours more grapefruit juice, takes off her glasses. 'I'd like to speak to mum about it. If you agree.'

'Why?' I know this family's far out, but I'm not sure sharing your love life with your girlfriend's parents is kosher.

'Because she said this would happen and when we were ready we could speak to her about being different.' I'm getting a bit narked with that phrase. It's making me feel a teeny weeny bit insecure. I may be only a teenager with limited experience, but I still have the old male pride that brings up defences when manhood is discussed. 'What do you think?' she asks. I munch some more breakfast, gulp coffee down too quick and splutter.

'I think we should do whatever we can.' I love it when I surprise myself. All that matters is I'm with this girl. I'll do anything. I could muck it up, get lairy, say nuts to Lilly, we'll be alright, or I could jump in head first, try and learn something. If there's anything to learn. We decide not to make love, wait till we speak to Lilly. There's a strange feeling between us. We've put the spotlight on full beam. There's no running away; it has to be looked at before we can go on. Here it is. Facing *The Big Lie*. It's haunted me all my days, and now it's here I can almost see why people run from it. Almost. I go to the bathroom and nearly puke.

Forty-Seven

When I get to Easton's in the afternoon, I'm wallowing in the joy of thinking I've found my voice. Poetry's never been my thing. I've always found it poncey. I was having a right mare until I had this idea. It doesn't have to rhyme, it can be a dialogue. It can be anything. So I spent a couple of hours after breakfast writing about me and Abigail and the *being different* conversation. I changed the names, made the characters a bit older, tried to be as honest as I could, and I'm well pleased with the results. I've been reading quite a lot of Hemingway, love the way he writes. He takes you with him. His writing's not obvious, not surface. He writes knowing his readers are intelligent, don't have to be spoon-fed. There's a sort of *going together* somehow, as if he's writing it with you.

Easton opens the door and peers over his horn-rims. He hasn't shaved, looks rough and is holding a crumpled page of writing with red scribbles all over it.

'Oh ... It's you. I suppose you'd better come in.' It's dark in the house, messy. No sign of Samantha. I'm getting fear tingles, wondering if he's murdered her, buried her in the garden. That's the trouble with imagination. Most of the time it's so daft.

'Tea, coffee, lager?' He's in his robe and pyjamas with leather slippers that squeak as he shuffles. The kitchen table's covered in unwashed plates, leftovers, the sink is full. 'I'm afraid things have gone to pot as you can see. Samantha's left me, the cow. Wanted to take Choo Choo, can you imagine? Take my baby.' He's filling the kettle and trying to clean up, badly. There's no sign of the dog. I tell him to go and sit down, he does so without argument. He keeps talking as I tidy up, make some coffee.

Choo Choo turns up through the back-door flap looking well miffed and quite nervous. I feed the little tyke. He tucks in ravenously. I'm wondering when he last ate. I take the coffee through to the study where Easy's rummaging through bits of paper on his desk. All of the pages are scribbled on with red marker. A homework teacher gone mad. He picks a page at random, almost spits at it. Seems they had a row over it, whatever it is.

'The trouble with modern writers is they think they can shortcut the greats and explore their navels with Tom, Dick and Mary. They can, of course, they do, and very successful in their creations some of them, but at what price, Naseem? Is the dumbing down of brother public so easy to overlook in the desire for fame and material gain?' I let him rant. Sit there while he goes on about literature having lost its heart, until he stops and starts to bawl. I'm at a loss. After a few seconds he apologises, tops up his glass of whisky and continues, as if nothing's happened, about Graham Greene being the last great English novelist.

There's something about the scene that doesn't hang together. It's as if he's writing his latest novel in real life. It's not going well. It's predictable, full of clichés, needs a good edit. I'm open to this man. He's as solid a geezer as I've met, but when the cards are on the table, he's just a bloke with a past like the rest of us, with all his demons. At the moment they seem to be crowding him into a corner. I don't say anything. Don't mention how obvious it is Samantha worships him.

Two hours later I leave him in his bed, well out of it, having emptied half a bottle of Glenfiddich. I'm a bit concerned, decide to come round tomorrow. He mumbles something about Samantha being *A puerile pleb who doesn't know the difference between a gerund and a ... synecdoche.* Ah, love.

Forty-Eight

Samuel's cleaning out the swimming pool when I get back. Shorts and T-shirt with sunnies. I grab the other pole and do my bit. By this time we're starting to get friendly, but I reckon there's a side he keeps well close to his chest.

'How you doing?' he asks. I tell him the usual, where I've been and other chunter. He jabbers about how well I'm doing, taking extra lessons, asks about the kitchen work.

'It's pretty grim,' I tell him. 'I'm thinking of doing what my mate Johnny's done and slide into the waiting game. It seems like fun, quite hard work, but there's a sort of flair that I like. It's a performance.' Samuel's quite young for a rich geezer, about forty-five I reckon. Well-built, quite good looking, a bit of a Robert Redford, but his accent's a bit soft, delicate, if you know what I mean. We finish getting the leaves out and start walking back to the house.

'Abigail's gone to her drama class, I expect you know. I was wondering, Naseem, have you got a few minutes?'

'Yeah, of course.' I follow him into his study. He sits down on this fancy black-leather sofa that goes around in a huge semi-circle about the size of mum's kitchen. I'm on a similar one but smaller. The study is a huge dome, with walls full of revolving bookcases, filled not only with books but all sorts of weird and wonderful tat. Works of art, obviously, but other things, jars with God knows what in them, animals, plants. About thirty feet up, through the top of the dome, is a smaller one, all glass. Looks like a telescope up there. There's a huge telly, part of the décor and desks, which appears to go up and down into the floor.

'The thing is, Naseem, you're almost one of the family, you fit with us very well. I'd like to make you an offer. Don't panic. I'm not trying to buy you off or tell you to leave Abigail alone. I thought you might be interested in a proposition. What would you say ... to working for me?'

I'm looking at him, wondering what's going down. I'm really getting to like the man. He's allowed me into his home, a lairy teenager he knows nothing about, I'm living with his underage daughter and he wants to give me a job. He must see how I'm feeling, as before I get the nous to say anything he comes back with more.

'I understand how this must seem strange. Naseem, I'd like us to be good friends. I think we're already heading that way. After all, you and Abigail are close, and although you're both young, I'm not concerned about that. I've lived my life by letting things happen. Most people live frightened lives because they desperately hold on to what they have.' He waits for a bit, letting that sink in. 'I know you're not interested in most of the school side of things, but you love dancing, English, basketball and are starting to enjoy philosophy.' By this time, I'm in a daze. I ask him how he knows so much.

'Abigail tells me everything. That's part of our deal,' he says and relaxes into the sofa.

'Is André following us everywhere also part of the deal?'

'Naseem, you must understand, I love my daughter. I don't want her hurt, but I have my reasons for allowing her to do what she wants. You're both very young. When Abigail spoke about her feelings for you, we agreed on a plan, as long as you were both sensible and … she told her mother and me everything. She's told you about her condition. We've always done our best to treat her as someone who's perfectly healthy, and for many years she has been. There's no reason to believe it won't continue to be that way, but we can't help being concerned it might recur. Naseem, we don't know for certain, and because of this Lilly and I decided to allow her to experience whatever she desires, within reason.' I'm sat there with my mouth open, one of those guppy fish comes to mind. 'Please think about my offer, and if you agree, we can start after you finish school.'

'What is it exactly you want me to do?'

'First, it involves you using your intuition. Like when it's working on the basketball court.' I'm waiting for the knockout punch, but he doesn't deliver. That's it. He gets up, goes over to the french windows, says he'll see me at dinnertime.

Blown away, man. Blown away. I'm wondering what the hell he means about *using my intuition* as I walk over to the garage where André's just parked up. He nods hello and heads towards his gaff. Abigail jumps out full of buzz. We don't say anything, snog. She pulls back, looks at me, smiling.

'What?' I say.

'Been busy?' she asks. Funny how eyes can smile more than lips sometimes. 'Some people have nothing better to do than ponce about play-acting, having a laugh.' She breaks away as if we're rowing and heads towards the garden. Starts going down the steps.

'Some people are nasty and jealous,' I say in turn.

'Take your clothes off.'

'Take yours.'

Which one's me, which her, does it matter? There's a distinct black and white in the sky, a threatening chessboard that makes the patches of blue sharper. We run about in the lower garden. The summer house has become *Our House*. We call it *The Love Den*. Sick. I told you, I don't care. I'm sinking in syrup, plunging down the sickly sweet swamp of sugar-coated yuck.

Listen, all this might sound too much, right? A couple of kids behaving at times so adult and so daft. Come on, what about Romeo and Juliet? She was only thirteen. Christ, that's too young, man. That is weird and pervy. The thing is, we're all different. I swear, for a while I knew stuff when I was small that I shouldn't have. It didn't last. I lost it, whatever it was, became a normal, naive kid that needed love. Tough. The world's a mess. It's not Enid Blyton and Richmal Crompton. It's more Miller and Steinbeck.

'Naseem! Come back, Naseem!' We watched *Shane* a while back on the box, me and the Dambois gang. It was well old-fashioned. A cowboy film stuffed with heart and a fair bit of cringe. Alright, I guess. On the whole. Tugged the strings. Abbie and Lilly were flowing with the tears. Me and Samuel were keeping shtum, trying not to laugh. Shane wanders off into the sunset, bleeding from a bullet, and this little kid who loves him shouts, 'Come back, Shane!' Shane ain't having it. He's off to the mountains to croak. Well mythic. Ever since, whenever I'm off with the fairies, Abigail has a go.

'Naseem, come back!'

'Yeah, alright, girl. I'm not Billy Liar. I am here.'

'I do wonder sometimes. What's the matter?' I tell her about Easton. 'What can you do, Naseem? Apart from going round … seeing if he's okay. It's his life, their life.' I listen to her, know she's right, but can't help feeling anxious.

'I'm going back to see how he's doing. He was so drunk he could do himself a mischief. Not kill himself – I don't think he's that way, but … I don't know, fall over, leave the gas on.'

'Let's go.'

'You don't have to.'

'Come on, Shane.'

She runs off. I follow. She suggests André could take us, but, believe it or not, I don't find it easy being a lord, so we wait for a bus.

When we get there it's about six o'clock, and the front door's open. The place is a tip again, and he's in the garden, out of it, on the little patch of lawn beyond the patio with an empty wine bottle next to him. Choo Choo's licking his face. He looks like he's banged himself. Nothing bad, a bump and cut right in the middle of his forehead. Twerp. He's still compos, singing something and rambling, swearing at Samantha, begging her to come back. Choo Choo's overjoyed to see us. Abigail falls in love with the runt and feeds it.

'You filthy cow … Samantha, my love, you fiend in woman's form, I want you, come back … my darling little crumpet … my nemesis … heartless androgyne …' We get him into the lounge, onto the sofa. I'm glad Abigail's here because he's a dead weight. We clean him up, lie him on his side, let him sleep. Then we clean the house, which takes about an hour, and finally make a cup of tea. As we're about to sit down, there's a knock at the door. Samantha turns up. She looks confused, embarrassed. We go through the usual intro and sit there for a while in a noisy silence.

'I'm so sorry about everything – all this. What must you think? I've been … we've … I'm so glad you two came. Thank you for …' She's sobbing. Abigail sits next to her, puts her arm around her, tells her it's going to be alright just as Easton turns over and farts.

They'd had a row. It must have cut deep. The spark that sets a house on fire can be tiny. She'd had enough of the way they were living. The drinking was getting her down. She gave him an ultimatum. Her or the drink, one of them had to go. She went. She's been staying with a friend but couldn't help herself coming round to check on him morning and evening.

'I tried to clean up, but it made him angry. So I left it. Left everything. He wouldn't even let me feed Choo Choo. I tried to take him away, but he stopped me. Said they'd starve together. I don't know what to do. I'm praying he'll stop. There's nothing left for him to drink.' She's in a right state. We try to calm her down. I tell her I'll come every day and see how he's doing, make sure he's alright, feed the dog. After a while she seems better, gushes her thanks, says for us to go. Easy's snoring away with Hemingway and Fitzgerald.

214

We leave, head for the beach, run for the beach, and for a second, as I'm chasing Abbie, letting her go ahead, the thought of her past, the hole in her heart springs up. Christ, should I stop her running? Should I treat her with pathetic kid gloves? Should I stress about everything?

'Shane! Come back, Shane!'

Forty-Nine

There are so many massive experiences coming out of the ultraviolet with not a clown in sight with a clue how to handle them. Falling in love seems to be so weird, everyone wants it, or at least they dream about it. It's in our make-up. You can't deny it unless you're some dried-up priest or scientist, and I don't trust either of those bods. But let's face it, blokes haven't a clue about the 'L' word. There's the animal urge, and that's it. It's a natural need you don't think about, or think about all the time, but not what it actually is. It's something you do, enjoy if you can, whenever you can, as much as possible, without getting trapped in a duff relationship. Or if you do get trapped, make sure you have loads of fun on the side, have kids with *her indoors*, forget about her as anything other than a substitute mother (naff off, Freud), washerwoman, cleaner and, yeah, occasionally, out of the kindness of your heart, keep her happy with a kiss on the cheek, if at all.

How does a plum like me know about all this? Have a look around.

Most people's relationships are a lie. Look at your family, aunts, uncles, older mates. After the lovey-dovey loses its savour it all goes sour. The blokes have to put up with *her indoors*, her moods, and she knows. She knows you don't love her, that you hate yourself and her because you're both trapped, living the God-awful lie of having to be together. Why? Christ knows. Blokes go to war, build empires, land on the moon, but they can't deal with *her indoors*. She knows you're a fake and you know she's right. Nightmare. Maybe I'll find out when it goes belly up with Abigail.

The whole world's involved in a secret conspiracy not to talk about love. We had sex education at school. It was so pathetic. Thirty lads being told the mechanics of intercourse with diagrams that might as well have been the London sewage system. Not a word about feelings. Why not? Because you can't teach what you don't know, haven't experienced. Most of the guff they teach is all theory, so why not teach a theory of love?

It's too vast, I suppose, too intimate, personal. The idea that we can talk about things other than the mechanics is wild and whacky. No one talks about the fundamentals. *This is a man. This is a woman. This goes here.* That's it. That's sex education. Nobody knows how to talk about it because there's no language for it. No one explains what it is because they don't know. I'm starting to wonder if I'm losing it with all this, but I've never been in love before. *Making love.* It's not *Making sex.* Why is that?

I can't help looking at it, and it's starting to make me feel a bit weird. I'm dissecting it like those frogs in biology. There's a fear about it all. What happens to the love, the magic? Why

218

doesn't it last? I have this sense I'm on dangerous ground, that if I look too close it might vanish. Somewhere in the muck and mire of my brainbox there's a warning light going off. It's hidden under all those secret boxes, the unwanted, forgotten bits of junk. Old toys, furniture, photos of dead dogs, Arabs in some garden, all dressed in mufti, looking stern and something else. There's a knowing in their eyes, a sort of waiting.

I'm afraid it'll go. Let's face it, it can't last, can it? It's almost like I know it'll happen and I'm getting myself ready for it. Trouble is, it's doing my nut. A shadow's started to grow inside. I know it's there, know it's some part of me that I don't understand, and it wants to take over. I've been pretending it's not there, praying it's not there, praying that if I don't think about it it'll go away.

It doesn't.

My greatest fear ... *The Big Lie*. Am I going to be the same? Join all the rest, the chain-gang of millions who've signed on the dotted line and given up?

Fifty

Johnny's been avoiding me at work for the last few weeks. I hate to say it but I'm relieved. It's easier than pretending everything's alright. So when he rang out of the blue on Saturday my sirens were on alert. As he's gassing, I remember another dream I had about him recently. He was going through a rough landscape in an old banger, trying to get to me. His steering was useless. Somehow he was driving from the back seat, being chased by someone, something, that he couldn't see.

'Penny and me found a little place in town. Here, why don't we meet up in half an hour? How about Sorrento's? I'll get you a hippy salad for lunch.' I tell him I'll be there and hang up. When I arrive he's in the window seat, smoking. He grins and waves like the queen. Sorrento's is a trendy restaurant-cum-wine bar that does wonderful fresh food, salads, all sorts of healthy nosh. There seem to be a few of these upmarket hippy gaffs opening.

'Took your time, mate. I've had three Italian coffees and a rum baba,' he said and stubbed his fag out in an ashtray full of dogends.

'Why aren't you at work?'

'Same as you, Naz. I do get some time off. I'm in this evening. I prefer the night shifts, they go quicker. What you having?'

'A Coke will do.' He looks alright; perhaps he and Penny are going to be okay. He heads over to the counter, comes back with the drink and a massive piece of carrot cake, puts them in front of me, sits down.

'You look like you need some carbs. Been overdoing it, Naz? That's the trouble with new toys, innit? Can't get enough to begin with,' he says with a slimy smile. 'Come on, it's bean-spilling time. Give and take.'

I eat some cake, look at him, say nothing. We both know something. We've both had a bite of a hook that seemed to have been dangling over our heads for far too long. The delights of initiation, the stepping over a line you can never go back from.

'Johnny, if you think I'm going to share anything other than *Yes, I'm having an amazing time with Abbie*, you're sadly mistaken. There's nothing to say, it's too …' He leans over, takes the whole of what's left of the cake, stuffs it in his gob and slowly munches, looking at me all the while with knowing eyes. Smiling with such a huge mouthful of carrot cake is no easy feat, but he does it well.

'Careful you don't choke,' I say. He sputters, and some cake bits rocket over the table. We wipe it up, laughing. I ask about Penny, but he's giving less than me.

'We might take a little trip,' he says. He orders another coffee with his hand, lights up the last fag in his packet and leans back.

'Fancy coming? Be nice, four of us, somewhere scorching. Never been abroad, Naz. It'll be brilliant, widen the horizons. Remember Easy Easton banging on? *Travel broadens the mind, boys*.' Looking closer, I see Johnny has dark shadows under his eyes; his fingernails are bitten down to the skin.

'What's happening? Really?' He looks out the window, doesn't say anything for a while.

'Things change, Naz. We all change. I'm thinking about the future. I want something different. Me and Penny want more than this.' He went on about a new life and how it'd be great to all go together. It did sound appealing, and I told him I'd speak to Abigail. I don't think Johnny was talking about a couple of weeks on the Costa. There was a desperation almost, a nervousness I didn't like.

'You think Charlie's going to let you go?' I ask. He shifts uneasily. I can tell he is frightened, worried but trying to be cool.

'I don't give a monkey's, Naz. We're going and that's all there is. Penny's got money and I've saved a bit. Christ, I'd have thought you'd be pleased. Look at this place, it's dead, man. There's nothing here but growing old and playing the pools. Come on, Naz, take a chance.'

I don't feel good. My mate wants me to be with him, start a new adventure, and I am already in one. I can't help the selfish thoughts in my head. I want to be alone with Abigail, in our bubble. I can't explain that to Johnny, can't tell him I'm not interested in his new life with some gangster's daughter. I have bad vibes about the whole affair, but it's obvious he is too far down the road to listen.

'Naz, I've got to meet Penny in a minute ... but mate, I'm serious. Come with us. I know it's mental, but it'll be a laugh, it'll be totally amazing. I love you, man, you know that, and I'm so pleased, you know, you and Abigail ... Look, we're going down the Pigeon's Nest this Saturday. Be there, please. We can talk some more.' He looks drained when he leaves. I sit there watching him go down the high street. He turns around once and smiles.

Fifty-One

I'm about to get up and leave Sorrento's when someone hovers next to me. I look up, and there's Samantha. She's wearing the happy face I remember from our first meeting, the one that made me wonder about her and Easy. There's still the pain around the eyes that comes when *The Big Lie* drops for a few seconds, days, years, but she seems lighter somehow. A few weeks have passed since Easy's meltdown. She moved back in a few days ago, and I've stopped going around apart from Sundays.

'Samantha … hi.'

'Hello, Naseem.' She sits down, relaxes, looks around, gets her cigarettes out, lights one up. 'What are you doing here?'

'What are *you* doing here?' She laughs easily. We've been getting to know one another over this period. Easton's ego having taken a battering has allowed her to blossom a little. She's more relaxed, more confident. He nearly ended up in hospital with alcohol poisoning. I think she's enjoying looking after him.

'I often come here for lunch. My office is round the corner.'

'Can I get you anything?' I get her a coffee and wait. There's that something about her when someone has a secret they can't wait to tell but she's holding it in. 'How is he?'

'Much better. I've left him to his own devices while I do a bit of shopping.'

'Is that a good idea?' She pauses before answering.

'I don't know, Naseem. He's … different. I think he frightened himself this time.' She looks at me, and we're silent for a while. 'There's something else. You know I … I mentioned I'd written a novel.' She twirls the coffee spoon in the cup as she's saying this.

'Yeah – I can't wait to read it.' She stubs out the cigarette, delves into her satchel, brings out a manuscript, pushes it in front of me.

'Don't open it, please. Not now.' She gathers her things, starts to get up. 'I'd better go. He'll be getting anxious. Tomorrow?'

'Sure.' She kisses me on the cheek and leaves.

As soon as she's out of sight I head for the library and start reading. Surprise! The novel's about a fiery university professor and his adoring students. The funny thing about the manuscript are these red scribbles all over it. Then the penny drops. They're Easton's. It's what he was ranting about the day I went round and he was out of it.

I spend the next couple of hours reading it. It's quite tricky, a bit of a mind twister. Russian dolls that fit into each other. The young professor (obviously based on Easton) is witty, suave, at the top of his game. He's had success with a

226

first novel, praised by the literati. There's talk of a new star in the firmament, comparisons with the heavyweights. He's adulated by all the female students, apart from one (based on Samantha). She's different. Doesn't play the usual groupie game, keeps out of his limelight.

At a Christmas party in her second year he tries it on, and, although she likes him, she won't have it. She knows his reputation and has no intention of being a notch on his belt. He gets narked. The next term he starts making life difficult for her, finding fault in her work, putting her down in class. She knows what he's doing. She works hard and waits.

This is where it gets strange. A novel within a novel. The Samantha character writes a story about a womanising university professor. The professor is found in a cleaning cupboard with an under-age student. He gets suspended and finally, sacked. It doesn't end there. He spirals, goes on a blinder, ends up in hospital. It's in all the newspapers. His university career is over. No one visits. No one cares. Then the Samantha character turns up. Looks after him. Helps him recover, and gradually they fall in love.

After he's over the worst they decide to move to pastures new. A seaside town where she grew up. She gets a job as a journalist on the local paper, works her way up. All he can manage after his downfall is a teaching job. He pretends it doesn't matter. Says it'll give him the impetus to write. Only it doesn't. He's lost it. The flame. Years go by. He's getting a modest whack from his first book, but that's not the point. He's lost the magic, feels useless. Starts to drink. Quietly. To begin with it doesn't show, but as time chunters on he needs more. For a while he manages to contain it. It doesn't work.

The Samantha character knows. She's not stupid. Things get worse. He becomes jaded, cynical, at times violent. One day he wakes up and she's not there. On the kitchen table there's a manuscript.

The book ends abruptly. A cliff-hanger. Or perhaps it's unfinished. It leaves me wondering if the real Samantha gave it to the real Easton and when. How much of it is true, how much the fanciful dreams of a young woman besotted with a glamorous university teacher? Did Easton write a bestseller? Did he get sacked?

Fairy tales. Why is it they never end *Happily Ever After*?

Fifty-Two

Perhaps there's one of those hippy, cosmic alignments going on, something to do with the Age of Aquarius. Christ knows. Abigail's in hospital. She's fine, apparently, but had a fainting fit and is in for a check-up, observation. André's the only one at home and takes me to the hospital. On the way he asks me how she's been. I'm bricking myself, go into a blank.

'How has she been recently?' I don't hear him. I'm away with the demons, thinking it's my fault, thinking she could die, might be dead already and I'll have killed her. He sees I'm somewhere else, asks again.

'Fine,' I manage. 'We were running around on the beach the other day. She was fine ... fine this morning. Has this happened before?' He tells me it has a couple of times, but each time she gets better, stronger, and her folks are stuck in a place where they can't win. We're silent for the rest of the ride. When we get there I run into reception. Samuel's there. He's on his way out.

'She's okay, Naseem. We're going to have to sit down, work out where we go from here. It may be we do nothing different, we have to wait and see.' I'm choked, can't say anything. He leads me to Abigail's room and leaves. She's looking gorgeous. Her hair's draped on her pillow, she's smiling in her sleep. The old poison in my head tells me she's doing this on purpose. Wants the attention. She's never asked for anything in the time I've known her. Yeah, she's a rich man's daughter, but she could be anywhere and still be the same. Some people are lucky that way.

We take it in turns to stay with her over the next couple of days, and she's all uppity with it. Wants to get home. Seems cushty. I was given a pep talk by the doctor. She reckons Abigail's fine. No internal bleeding in her valves. The faint was probably to do with hormone levels. The upshot was to take it easy with the lovemaking, nothing strenuous for a few weeks, regular check-ups. I'm glad the doctor saw me on my own.

Fifty-Three

Giorgios, the restaurant manager, wants to know if I've seen Johnny. He hasn't been coming in. I tell him I don't have a number for his new gaff. I've not been going to work myself, what with Abigail, and I'm wondering what's happening. After I finish my day shift I head over to Johnny's. Penny opens the door. I introduce myself and ask how he's doing. She lets me in and makes a cup of tea.

'He's been trying to get hold of you ... when he's sober.' She seems a really nice girl. Tells me things have been going downhill with Johnny for a while. Her dad's been putting the pressure on them, threatening to get him roughed up. 'My dad's mental. He thinks he owns me ... I'm sick of it. Johnny's the best thing I've had in my life, and I don't want to lose him. We're thinking of going abroad but haven't enough cash. Dad's blocked all my bank accounts. Every time Johnny goes to work there're some of his heavies hanging around. They haven't actually done anything yet, but dad's given us an ultimatum.' She tells me she has to go home or they'll make life even worse. Johnny's been escaping into the booze.

I find him out of it in the bedroom. There's stuff around ... empty bottles, looks like he's been smoking dope as well. I go back to Penny in the lounge. She's watching vomit TV and chain-smoking. Penny's a looker, a natural blonde, thin, elegant, a sort of model look about her. She starts gassing about everything, I get the whole shebang. I was right, she's worked in London in some big fashion agency. Said they might have a chance if only her dad left them alone, but she's worried about Johnny's head. He's become paranoid, frightened of everything.

The long and short of it is they're up the creek. She's up the duff, in the club, petrified her old man will blow a fuse, do something mental if he finds out. I try to calm her down, say I'll do what I can to help. Christ knows why I said that. What can I do? Go and see her dad with a gun? Ask André to teach me kung fu in a couple of days? I tell her to let me know when Johnny wakes up and give me a ring. I leave with her in tears. The people I love are collapsing. There's nothing wrong with me. Why is that?

When I get back to Abigail's I don't mention anything about Johnny. She's making dinner and I help out. After a while the whole family's tucking in to noodles, all sorts of vegetables, fried tofu, beansprouts, fresh nuts, salad and wine for all. A feast. She's eating like a thoroughbred. I smile at her. She catches me looking.

'What?'

'Nothing.'

'How's work, Naseem?' Lilly asks. She's wearing an evening dress that must be Vietnamese. It's tight, slender, almost see-through, dangles to the floor. Her long hair is in a pyramid sort of shape that's up, showing her neck, and it has all these wooden sticks in it.

We gas about stuff. Samuel entertains with how Lilly and he met, fell in love. After dinner I wander outside, light a fag. Abigail comes up behind me, tugs my arm.

'You were late back from work.'

'Worried I'm seeing someone else?' She hugs me, pinches my bum. We snog.

'I went to see Johnny.'

'How is he?'

'Not too hot. Things are getting on top of him.' I leave it at that and throw the fag away. 'That's the last one ever.' She laughs at me. Right, that's it. It's done. Red rag to a bull and all that. 'Let's make a little wager. Fancy a flutter, Miss Dambois?'

'How awfully vulgar, but if it helps the lower classes, one must do one's duty. What did you have in mind, my good man?' I grab her close, tight, tell her I love her, everything about her, and if she ever has another faint, I'll kill her. We snog some more, and I realise we might be being watched, give it a rest.

'We heading for bed?' I ask in a whisper. She takes my hand and leads me on. When we get upstairs she says she's spoken to Lilly and she'll speak to us whenever we want. We have a bath together then jump into bed. We cuddle.

'Abigail ...'

'Yes?'

'We are ... different.'

'I know. Do you not want to see Lilly?'

'Yeah, I do.'

Fifty-Four

'I'd like to see my brother and sister, mum. It's not much to ask. I know I've never been much of a brother, but I still love them.'

'It's not a good time, Naseem.'

'When is it ever?'

'Naseem, I wasn't going to tell you yet, but your grandfather died recently and your dad's taken it badly.'

I can't make sense of anything. Here's the man who went home to Syria a few years back and sat with all the family around the dining-room table. Grandad on one end, Taras at the other and everyone else bricking themselves. He lays into his dad like a cut kipper, slices him open in front of his children and wife, says he wishes he was dead – that he'll dance and spit on his grave. I'm there with everyone else trying to be invisible. I'm thinking, Oh my Christ, why did I have to have this plank for a father? Now his old man's pegged it he suddenly feels something. Leave it out.

I don't make a fuss, say I'll catch up with Jamal and Iman after school or nursery one day. I ask her how she's coping, and she gives me the nightmare. It's always a nightmare with Taras. They'll have to go to Syria for the burial. Then it clicks. He's after the readies. Old grandad was a big nob in the government, had a few dinars. Cynical, me? On your bike.

'Oh, and Naseem, someone from the school phoned about your attendance. They said if you don't go in, at least for the English, you won't be able to take the exam. There are only three weeks left. I felt so bad making excuses for you, you little tyke. Oh, and the sports chap, Wendel? He phoned as well, asked if you could play basketball next Friday evening. It's the final.'

I jabber a bit more, try and make her laugh. It doesn't take much. All I need to do is mention Taras in a daft light and she's gone. It's bad talking about people behind their backs, evil. I tell her I love her, ask her to give the kids a hug. She tells me to go away and live my easy life.

The next couple of weeks I'm running about like a Tasmanian devil. Everything's coming together in some insane, demonic, circus act. Ducking and diving takes on a whole new meaning. In all the madness I find respite with Abigail. We take things slow. I'm a bit on eggshells, but she keeps trying to push me out of the worry, doing silly things for the sake of it. Thinks its funny. Last Saturday we went for a walk along Beachy Head. She kept running about pretending she was a bird. I tried to slow her down, grab her, hold on to her, she kept escaping, legging it. She wasn't overdoing it, it was all gentle stuff, but I still crapped myself.

The day before that she was going loopy at the basketball match, the county final. It was held at Sussex Uni in Falmer. The tip-off was five thirty. The lads all got there early to practise, and I managed to join them. It was good to have some time to warm up as I was so rusty. I haven't been going to the Wednesday-evening practice. What with work and everything else, basketball seems like a distant memory. Wendel, our coach, could see I wasn't as sharp as I used to be.

'When does it start?' she asked. Abigail looks the business. A satin blue dress that makes her look so much older than she is. The lads are having a break before the game. It's five o'clock.

'You know when. I've told you. You don't half look tasty.' The hall is nearly empty, only a couple of university lads messing about.

'Where have your team gone?' I explain, and she sees I'm anxious. 'What's the matter, Naz?'

'I'm useless … haven't practised. I don't think I'm going to make the first five.' As I'm saying this Wendel comes along. I introduce Abigail. He tells me what I expected: he'll bring me on as a sub … if I'm needed. With that he heads off to the changing room, says to come along when I'm ready for the pep talk.

'Abigail, I've got twenty-five minutes to pull myself together.' She gives me a kiss, and I head towards the lads shooting hoops. I ask if they'll help me out. For the next twenty minutes we play one-on-one. They're big lads and they're good. I start out lame, have to take a breather. I'm so glad I'm giving up the fags, but it's doing me in not having trained. I hammer it with the uni lads, who really make me graft. After ten minutes I'm starting to come back, and in the final five I'm holding my own, almost back to scratch. By

237

now the place is filling with students who've come to watch, and the players of both teams are out warming up. I do the opposite, tell Wendel I'm going to the loo and head out onto the football pitch. I start jogging. I know I'm not going on first, so I spend another ten minutes doing circuit training, pushing it, then stretch and rest. I go back in. We're losing badly.

I wave to Abigail, who's sitting in the front row to the left of the official's table. I head for our bench and take a seat. The score is fifteen-six to Dorothy Stringer School; they look sussed. They're a good team with a coach that knows his onions. They love the game and don't ponce about. Wendel calls a time-out when Matthew gets fouled. He gives some spiel about working together, keeping it tight defensively. Useless. The lads are looking at me, and I'm sat there. There's nothing I can do. I try and encourage them, but they're dragging it. Their hearts are down by their feet. It's not happening. There are five minutes left of the first half.

Matthew pulls a few back, but he's doing it on his own. Dorothy Stringer know it's in the bag and are taking it easy. The whistle goes for half time with the score on twenty-four to twelve. Michael Braithwaite, our pivot, has twisted his ankle, and my heart starts beating fast. This is my chance. Wendel grabs Garry Dean, an overweight lad who's full of enthusiasm but absolutely useless, and tells him he's on. I'm getting angry now. I know Wendel's doing this because I haven't been to practice. Fair enough, I suppose.

It's going downhill. Stringer are messing about like it's a holiday. There are ten minutes left and we're still twelve points behind. I keep looking at Wendel, but he's not having it. There's a foul called on Stringer, and Matthew goes over to Garry, whispers something to him. Garry starts holding his stomach, moaning. Good old Charlie. I look at Wendel, who knows something's up, but he waves me on.

Straight away Matthew and me are magic, on fire. Tom Ansell, our right-attack, clicks into gear, catching the flame. We pull six points back. The team sense we're back in gear, start getting sharp. It only takes a new breeze to change a sad direction. Stringer are a bit fazed. They think they're still okay as there are six points between us and are messing about, keeping the ball too long. Stevie and Danny are playing a blinder all of a sudden in defence, feeding the forwards on the rebound. Matthew shoots two lovely baskets, bringing us back to two behind. Three minutes on the clock. Stringer call a time-out. Wendel's having a heart attack with the excitement, makes no sense with his gabble and shoves us back out. I call them around quick, we circle, do the hands and shout, 'Dorothy Stringer, here we come!'

I fly down right in my favourite position when I see Stevie fall over and scream. The ref blows his whistle. The clock stops on two minutes forty-five. Stevie's so messed up with it, he's sobbing as he's helped off. Garry comes back on looking scared, bricking it. I tell him to float, and he says, 'What's that?' I explain he doesn't defend, stays near their end line, waits for the ball. He looks at me confused. I tell the others to pull a diamond half-court press, and we're away. Stringer have the ball, keeping it, so we press them. Two minutes left, and I call *seventeen*. We press the man with the ball. It's a big risk because there are only four of us in our

239

half of the court. If he stands his ground, makes a good pass, it's over. He fumbles. Tom drives all the way.

Wendel's screaming for Harry to get back and defend, but I wave him away. I look at Matthew, and we head away from the ball, giving Stringer's forward a chance to drive. I shout at Danny and Tom to let them through. This confuses Stringer as we're open, but in that second of confusion Matthew and me surround the ball man and hassle. The clock's on one-minute ten, and we steal it. Matthew lobs it down the hall to Garry who doesn't know what to do for a second. Stringer haven't guarded him because they know he's naff, and Garry manages to score just before he's swamped. He's elated. We're all square. I look around for Abigail, and she's jumping and … mum and the kids are there.

We won. We stole it. Stringer were all over the shop. We had them on a full-court press. They tried to dribble out of it. One little mistake, and Tom lobs it to Matthew who flies down the right, and that's it. The whistle's gone and the lads are manic. There's a small crowd of spectators giving it all they've got, up and shouting like banshees. We did it. I run over to Abigail who jumps on me. I tell her my mum's here with the kids and we go over, say hello. I give Iman and Jamal hugs and kisses. For once, they actually look like normal kids having fun.

Fifty-Five

'Hey, Naz, good to hear your voice, man.' It's Johnny. It's two in the morning. Abigail looks up with one eye closed, and I wave to her it's alright. I throw a dressing gown on and take the phone onto the balcony. The sky's a star-speckled black cloak with a sliver of yellow moon laughing at me. Johnny sounds a bit groggy.

'Johnny, you alright?'

'Yeah, man, I'm magic. Sorry I was out of it when you popped over. Listen, you mustn't worry about me, brother. I'm doing fine. Sorry it's so late. I wanted to tell you that Penny's old man, he's come round, man. I can't believe it, Naz. He wants me and Penny to live at his mansion, in an annexe. I don't understand it. I'm a bit worried he might be laying a trap, you know, man. It's been a bit mad, Naz. I've been out of it ... losing it ... recently. I didn't want to worry you.' He sounds shaky. I'm wondering if it's all more vomit talk.

'You could have told me tomorrow, you plank. Nah, listen, man, I'm blagging ya, I'm over the moon. What's the next move?'

241

'I'm not sure, Naz.' He goes quiet and I'm wondering what's happening.

'Johnny? What's up?'

'It's Pete, Naz, my father ... he's gone, mate. We've only now got back from the hospital. He collapsed a few hours ago. He's gone, Naz. He was my dad, you know – he was a blinder. Mum's in a state ... She's here, with me and Penny. The doctor's given her a sedative.' I listen, hear his pain, I know it's hard for him to share this. His family has always been his rock. Being fostered from the age of seven, they've loved him like their own. I try to say something, but I'm a bit stumped.

'Want me to come round?'

'No, Naz. I needed to speak to you, man. I miss you, bro. We need to get together, like the old days.' There was a silence that went on for too long. He choked up, said he was sorry, said he'd give me a bell another time and put the phone down.

The moon's still laughing at me. There are seven or eight little puffs of cloud along the horizon lit up by the moon. A train on its way to Neverland. I wish it would stop and take me to the Wild Boys. Books should be banned, burned to Fahrenheit 451. I love them, hate them. Maybe they're all part of *The Big Lie* as well. They fill you with wonder, with dreams. Dreams you pray will never end, dreams that tell you anything's possible and then reality comes along. Reality kicks you in the belly. Reality hits you with a massive great hammer and says, 'Wake up, you plum. This is misery land, and you're going to suffer.' Reality laughs its head off, runs away skipping into the invisible. We're all silly dreamers who have to wake up.

I leave Abigail snoring softly and wander out into the garden. There's something about the shining crescent up there that grabs hold of me. All those stories of lunatics, people being affected by cosmic vibes, can't all be old wives' tales. I've got a coat over my pyjamas but it's still a bit chilly. I'm about to go back in when I see her, Lilly. It must be about half-two. She's dressed in white silk pyjamas, under a white fur coat draped over her shoulders with matching hat. Looks like a fairy. For a minute I'm not sure if she's real. She has that effect. She doesn't say anything, comes over to where I am. A geisha hovering about. She looks up at the moon.

'There is a Vietnamese story about a man in the moon,' she says. The tale is a bit long-winded, goes on about a magic healing tree, a sick beautiful maiden who accidentally chopped its root. The tree starts floating away. Hubby comes home, tries to grab the floating tree, and it takes him to the moon. Fairy tales get on my wick. Why do they have to be so silly? Everyone knows what's going to happen and what you should or shouldn't do, and the idiots always do it anyway.

'So he's still up there? Must get lonely on his own,' I say.

'Perhaps he likes to be alone.' She walks back towards the house. 'I'm making some lemon-and-ginger tea; would you like some? It's very soothing.' I follow her into the kitchen, perch on one of the stools near the bar.

'The moon is a powerful magnet. It can help with deep meditation.' It's three in the morning, and I'm chatting to my girlfriend's mum about meditation.

'Why do you meditate, Lilly?'

'To be one with my true being. You wish to know what that is?' I nod, and she carries on while getting the tea

243

together, chopping fresh ginger, grinding lemon rind and some other stuff that looks like spring onions. No. Can't be. 'Everyone has two realities. The outer and the inner. Most people are not aware of inside but inside is far more important. Outside will fade, grow old, die, but inside is immortal.'

I love it. Love the way she tells it without preaching. It's simple and makes me wonder. She does that. Gets me wondering. I wonder what she thinks, what she's like with Samuel. It's not that I fancy her. I don't. It's more than that. Some people aren't real. They're mythical. Easton calls them *archetypes*. Half the time I don't have a clue what he's talking about. God knows what my fellow Epsilons think … if they do think, that is. A lot of the time a sixteen-year-old's brain is not geared up for it. It's more a garbage bag of sexual ignorance meshed into a web, a twisted amalgam of erotic sweets. The book-reading seems to be affecting my waxing and waning. Maybe it's a natural progression.

'How's the lovemaking?'

'Sorry?' I say, spluttering some of the hot ginger tea.

'Abigail has told me that you are ready to talk. You must have some notion by now that this family is not quite normal. You know we discuss everything.' She's made some toast from crusty bread and topped it with honey and cream. Her movements are balletic. She seems to be able to enjoy the most ordinary things in a way I'd never thought possible. Yeah, she's … what's the word? Disconcerting. The swingometer's way off the scale.

'I don't really know what to say.' I'm trying to think of escape routes, but she's too quick.

244

'Let me help. You are unsure of your feelings. You are fearful you may lose your love for her.' I stare at my plate. The yellow of the honey and cream are looking up at me with a sort of smirk. They're grinning at my flush. Colours can be overbearing sometimes.

Lilly's a Daoist. I've heard the word but never chased it. I love the unfamiliar. It makes my flesh tingle, and I open up. My senses seem to be eager in a way that's mental. *Give me. Give me all of it. I want more.* So what is it? Daoism? I can't tell you. No. Listen, I can't tell you. That's it. Only it isn't. Sounds daft. There's this thing that is behind, inside, appearing as everything. It flows out of time and space. The purpose is harmony and the thing is the balance between the feminine and the masculine, only it's not only men and women. It's everything, and it can't be defined. Simple. Love it, man. Outta sight. Lilly explains all this in her disconcerting way and then keeps shtum.

'Why are you telling me all this, Lilly?'

'You are correct. You will lose your sexual desire for Abigail, and it will cause you tremendous heartache, confusion. At your age, this is natural. There are many reasons why a crossroads appears at a certain point. It may be you are ready, even at your age, to learn what may take another person many lifetimes.' I'm in, man. I'm Dirty Harry waiting for Lilly to *Make my day*.

Fifty-Six

I really want to take the English exam, so I go in on the Monday. Some young bloke's stepped in for Easton and the lads are giving him grief. He's such a hippy. Thin hair, parted in the middle, down to his shoulders; thick-lens glasses that make his eyes look massive, like they're popping out. Dark-brown flared cords and a flowery shirt. It doesn't bode well. Plus, have a laugh, he's called Mr Percy. Oh dear.

The deputy head must have sussed and comes in as the lads crescendo with expletives and start chucking things at the new boy. Silence falls as soon as he opens the door. Stan Merton takes no prisoners. He is absolutely mental, man. He doesn't show any emotion, that's why he's called *The Lizard*. He's fair but loves to cane. He lays six with his cold, deathly poison about behaviour and how he won't tolerate blah, blah, blah and threatens the whole class with detention.

Percy's alright. He asks if we want to do writing exercises or read. The choice seems daft. Turns out Percy's sussed. He gets the class to take it in turns reading from this book by some geezer called Stephen King. It's called *Carrie*. It's a belter, man. No bull, it blows the lads away. We get through the first few chapters in no time. The afternoon whizzes past. The writing's so easy, enticing, makes me think about giving up. How will I ever get close? But another part of me tingles with it. It's all I want.

After school I stop off to see how Easton's doing and give Samantha her manuscript. She opens the door, smiles, grabs it out of my hand and rushes off to the kitchen.

'He's upstairs in bed. Would you take him this coffee?' She's avoiding eye contact. I put her out of her misery.

'I loved it. It's not something I'd normally read, but I did, I loved it. Why isn't it published?' I sit on one of the stools while she hovers about.

'You tell me. Come on, Naseem … Use that writer's creativity, insight.'

'Too close to the bone?'

'No. It wasn't that. I could have used a nom de plume.' She looks away. Holds something in. 'I wrote it for him, for that time, because I loved him, because I wanted to reach him. I thought perhaps he might listen … might see me, see how different I was from the rest, fall in love with me. Stupid, right? How desperate. A silly, naive twenty-year-old, besotted with a successful, glamorous professor.'

'So? Come on … what happened?'

When she finished the novel she gave it to him. He was condescending, said he'd look at it when he had some spare time. Well, that was it as far as she was concerned. She got her degree, came down to Brighton, got on with her life. What happened next? More or less as she wrote it. It took another year or so for him to get sacked, but that's where

248

real life stepped in. He didn't go on a blinder. Instead, he looked for her, found her. She told him to get lost, said she wasn't interested, she'd moved on. He persisted. It took him six months to wear her down. That was fifteen years ago.

It turns out he'd only recently read the manuscript. He'd found it by accident while looking for alcohol. It was unopened, in a drawer in his study. The truth of it was too much for Easton. He lost it. Started drinking with a vengeance. That's when Samantha gave him the ultimatum.

'Far out, man,' I say. Life and fiction snuggling up. Magic. 'But that was then, surely now ...'

'It doesn't matter now, Naseem. Here, take this up to him. He wants to ask you something.' I take the coffee and head upstairs. My head's trying to make sense of what I've just heard. I nearly fall over with the coffee, knock on the bedroom door and wait.

'Come in, Naseem.' Well weird to see my English teacher in bed. Feels a bit dodgy. He looks a lot better, a bit tired but pleased to see me. I sit and chunter about stuff: Mr Percy, basketball, Henry Miller's *Tropic of Capricorn*. He loves it.

'Listen, Naseem, I'd like to thank you for all you've done and sincerely apologise for my behaviour of late.' I try to cut in, but he won't have it. 'I've decided to take early retirement. I've got a good deal, and Samantha and I – we're getting married. I'd like you to be my best man.' I look at him, and he's straight up.

'Me, your best man? I'm sixteen!'

'What's that got to do with it? Alright, best *young man*, how's that? Would you?'

'Far out, man. I mean, yeah, of course ... but, are you sure?'

249

'I'm sure.' He closes his eyes as if he's going to sleep. Samantha's right, he is different. Perhaps it was the fear of dying, but I don't think so. It was her novel. I reckon it reminded him of who he was, who he could still be. I get up to leave. As I'm going, he calls me back. Without opening his eyes he says he wants me to write a diary.

'What sort of diary? Day-to-day stuff?'

'No. I want you to start it when you were about twelve, right up until now. A journey of your discoveries, experiences, maturation. A wonderful chance to explore these seminal years of your life.' It sounds interesting. I ask how long should it be – a couple of pages?

'No, Naseem. I want you to write a book.'

Fifty-Seven

Summer's doing a runner. The rains have come with July, and Abigail wants to go away for her birthday. I'm up for anything, man. It's a whirlwind kind of happening that's laying down its psychedelic tongue all the way to my medulla oblongata. No, I haven't taken any psychedelics lately. Sometimes I look back and wonder what happened to the twelve-year-old kid. He was a right plum. Nice in a naive way, I suppose, but times move on, my man, times move on.

'Where do you want to go?' I'm brushing her hair … take a gander. She's sat in front of her boudoir painting her nails for a laugh. She doesn't normally go for the glam, and I have to say I like it that way. All the make-up bints slap on makes me nervous. It's animal war paint. Sex and violence. What happens when it comes off? Once they put it on they look like someone else; when it's gone – naked and helpless.

'Paris.'

'When?'

'My birthday's in four weeks.'

'The thirtieth?'

'Yes.'

'That's a Sunday.'

'How do you know that, Mr Al-Yawer?'

'Because the day before we're invited to a wedding.' She stops painting, blowing on her nails and looks at me in the mirror.

'I'm not marrying you, Naseem. Not yet.'

'Thank God for that. It's Easy Easton and Samantha. I'm the best man.'

'Isn't there an age limit for being a best man?'

'No. Crazy, innit?' I tell her about Samantha's novel. How she saw what was going to happen. How she had the courage to give it to him and leave.

'Hell hath no fury …'

'Like a woman who loves.'

'Do you think they'll last?'

'Who knows? Maybe. People settle for the devil they know. It's lonely being on your tod, and if it's alright some of the time …' She turns and hugs me around my waist.

'Please don't talk like that, Naseem. Not even as a joke.' She's crying. Not bawling, not sobbing, a couple of tears rolling down her lovely face. She gets up and takes off her dressing gown, starts getting dressed. We're going out, a foursome with Penny and Johnny. It's what happens. Another one of those rites. The blokes chat about football and the girls laugh at their blokes, watch them like hawks, see if they're eying up other bints. It's the slippery road to marriage, kids, a fat belly and living death. Cynical, me? Anyway, it'll be a good chance to see how Johnny's coping. It's only been a few weeks since his father pegged it, but

252

he sounded okay when we spoke on the blower a couple of days ago.

We made a blood pact when we turned fourteen. Debbie Mellison had broken his heart after three months of deep snogging and I'd had a sort of thing with a girl from Norway, Andrea. She was magic. Beautiful, blonde and raring. I stopped dancing for three weeks that summer. All we did was get into JoJo's, find our little alcove, get randy. It never went further than second base. Secretly, I was always glad. Even then I didn't have the bottle. I was saving it for Abigail.

Anyway, the Norway bint was only here for a few weeks. Still hurt like a bullet when she went, though. So Johnny and me got tight with a bottle of whisky in the park after a rough night dancing, trying to forget by remembering. How sad and silly is that, eh? People think only girls suffer from all the heartache stuff, but it's not true. We hammered it, cut ourselves with glass and made an oath. Christ what a couple of pillocks. We were crying like babies all night. Well, a couple of hours anyway. The oath was something about never getting stuck with one bint and having it away with as many as we could by the time we were twenty-one. Funny how things turn out.

The Pigeon's Nest is heaving. Johnny's piling on the drinks, acting lairy, and Penny's looking sad. It's obvious things are not tickety-boo. I take him aside to one of the tables that circle the upper landing of the disco bar. He looks at me, tries to smile, but it doesn't wash.

'What's going on, Johnny?' He doesn't answer straight away. He looks at all the boys and girls getting down. I can tell he's hankering.

253

'I miss it, Naz. The scene, the brothers. I miss being with you, the two of us, being on the prowl. Miss the sounds, the dancing, man. Once you're with someone, it all changes. It's gone, all that ... sparkle ... the dreams. You must know what I mean.' He swigs his lager and lights up.

'It's your life, Johnny. It's only just starting. It's not like you have to do anything you don't want.' He laughs, almost hysterical. Punters nearby look on and see the usual, a pissed-up clown who'll end the night in the gutter. I try and get him to calm down, keep the lid on it, but he's on a roll. There are people all around, but he's loud, almost shouting.

'She's having an abortion. Her old man's got inside her head, Naz. We're moving into the annexe in a few weeks. He told her he'll cut me up unless she lets it go. Funny thing is, Naz, I want it. I want the naffing baby. I've been thinking about it all really clearly.' He shoves his chair closer, wraps an arm around me. 'I'm about to tell you something, Naz. It hurts me to say this, but it's true. Me and you, we're blood, man, we're closer than blood ... but it's all gone, man. It's all drifted away, and I want something for me, Naz.' I could smell the stench of deep alcohol on his breath. Nothing had changed. If anything, he seemed more lost, rambling. He said he had a plan. He was going to kill Charlie and take his crown. Said he knew I didn't believe him, that I thought he was a drunk who was talking tosh, but he'd prove everyone wrong. Whatever he was on seemed to be kicking in. I took all he was saying like he said it. He was a drunk talking tosh. Finally, he looked at me and smiled, but it wasn't the smile I'd always remembered.

254

'Remember our oath, Naz? Look at us now, a couple of married blokes. Another drink?'

'They're going down fast, Johnny. You sure?'

'Lay off, man. Come on, I'm asking that poncey DJ for some funk.' He heads over to the bar and I swan back to the girls. I'm thinking of calling it a day. The night's not going well. Johnny's too far gone, and I've had enough of the old ways. It's almost perfect really. The time has come to walk out of the dance, walk out on my mate. Let him go. I'm ready for it. There's an iciness in my stomach that's steeled. I'm about to speak to Abigail when the sounds change down a gear, she takes my hand, leads me to the dancefloor. We get close with Billy Paul's 'Me and Mrs Jones'. She asks what's wrong. I say nothing. She knows, though.

The song ends and the sounds shift back to top gear. Too quickly. Must have been Johnny's doing. Maybe he slipped the DJ some wonga. The Godfather's screaming, telling everyone we need *Soul Power*. I catch Johnny dragging Penny through the crowd, and she's not happy about it. He's bumping, shoving, spilling glasses. Punters are starting to stare. Abigail's saying something in my ear, but I can't make it out. I can guess, though. The dance crowd starts getting the upbeat vibe, and the place gets funky. Then it happens. Bound to really. Some equally unhappy plank has had enough of Johnny's silly face and lamps him.

The trouble with bouncers is they don't care what happens outside. As long as everything's tight and tasty inside, they're happy. They grab the drunken idiot, my mate Johnny, and toss him out. Thing is, they throw everyone involved in the tussle. Both sides. The drunken idiot, my mate Johnny, wants to finish the job. Luckily there's a taxi outside, and I shove him in before he gets mashed.

Johnny falls asleep in the taxi. Penny's distraught, trying to play it down, saying he'll be fine in the morning. We drop them home, decide to go for a walk along the prom. We hold hands, walk in silence. It's a warm night and the sea's making love with the moon. We take our clothes off and join them. There's no one about at three in the morning.

We forget everything. Forget we're sixteen. Forget the baby that might never be born. Forget Johnny and Penny. The icy water brings back the life, brings back the place we know and love. I make a mental note that I can't see Johnny anymore. I love him, but he's in a dark hole and I can't help. I can't help my best mate. I have to let him go. I hate it, but I feel free somehow. I'm so right with this girl and I'm not letting anything come between us. Christ, I'm so selfish. Life's a bowl of ... snakes.

Fifty-Eight

My first wedding, and I'm up for the speech. There are about forty guests in this massive marquee. It's tipping it, but the sun's promising. Summer rain always makes me want to dance naked for some reason. I'm dressed in my best natty gear, looking the dog's. So's Abigail. I look at her and wonder who she's with, some loaded jerk who'll break her heart, turn her mumsy, keep her as an heirloom. Good thing she's with me. Easy and Samantha are glowing. Choo Choo has a new coat and collar.

I do the speech as best I can, and it goes down okay. Kept it short and sweet, no cheese. Abigail brings me some champers, and we snog away from the crowd.

'Well done, Nazzy.'

'Fancy a stroll?'

We're in the grounds of a country house in Steyning. It must cost a bomb, all this marrying lark. Can't see the point. The rain stops, and we wander into the gardens. The sun comes down hot and bouncy, changes the place in a few minutes. Everything's steaming with the heat. There's a little stream at the end of the garden with a path that goes on to what looks like some woods.

'Nazzy ...'

'Yeah?'

'I've been thinking of going to drama school again.' We'd spoken about the possibility, but it was only that.

'Amazing, Abbie. Somewhere in London?'

'Possibly. What do you think?' She seems unsure of herself. Perhaps she's worried I might be upset. 'I've done well with my exams and could go on to do A levels for another two years and then university.'

'Or?'

'Or I could go to a private drama school from September.' We stop walking and she looks at me, wanting me to say something. I tell her she has to do whatever she wants, especially as she's such a good actress.

'What are you worried about?' I say. 'London's only an hour away by train. It'll be far out. What do your mum and dad think about it? Have you spoken to them?' She tells me her folks would rather she stayed at home for a few more years, and I can understand, what with her heart condition.

'I'm not sure, Naseem. I feel I've had enough of education, but it may not be the right time. I want to be near you, always.' I take her hands and bring her in to me.

'Listen, Abbie, I'm not going anywhere. Whatever you want to do is okay as far as I'm concerned.' We walk back to the party, which is picking up with a band playing jazz. She gets me to dance. I do, but it doesn't come easy, all that loop the loop stuff, but we have a laugh.

I look around for Easton, see him chatting with some woman in a red dress under a red umbrella. Well glamorous. He calls me over, does the intro, sneaks off to find Samantha.

The woman in red is called Jemima. Turns out she's his publisher. Easton's given her the spiel about me being a writer. She doesn't look impressed.

'What's your style, Naseem?' I'm thinking about giving her some lip but stop myself, say I haven't found my voice. She looks at me and smiles. 'Harry seems to think you have promise. He likes taking young people under his wing. I trust my brother's writing judgement. It's about the only thing about him I do.' She looks away at Easy who's dancing with Samantha. 'Do you think it'll last?' she asks, as if she's known me for years, and I'm wondering what she's after.

'You're the second person who's asked me that. I do, as it happens. They're smashing. A bit mad, but hey.' She ganders me up and down, making up her mind.

'Have you read his book?'

'He never told me he'd written anything.' She lights up a menthol, goes quiet for a bit.

'Writers are often secretive. It's a dangerous profession. Precarious.' The sun comes out briefly to the left and the rain showers to the right. Everything's sparkling. I see Abigail dancing with some old geezer. 'There's a phrase in the business called a *One-Hit Wonder*. It can make or break a writer. Think of Salinger, Harper Lee. They may have written other works but are only ever remembered for the one and spend the rest of their lives either in its shadow or forever chasing it. It can drive people mad. Some find solace in drink, others become reclusive. Most settle for a faded glory and write rubbish ever after.' I could tell she was fond of Easy. She was looking at him all the while she was speaking. 'Well, I must go.' She put her hand out for me to shake. 'Goodbye, Naseem. Send me some

259

of your work. If you dare.' I watch her trundle off under her red brolly in her red dress. Publishers. Well dramatic.

I walk over to the bandstand where Samantha's sitting alone eating a large slice of wedding cake. It's getting late, the guests are starting to leave. She seems nervous. I give her a hug, ask how she's doing. She's worried.

'What's wrong?'

'Nothing. That's the point. He's doing so well. He hasn't touched a drop of alcohol and wants me to try and publish my book.'

'That's wonderful, Sam.'

'Yes, but for how long?' She's right, of course. It's all too quick, too good to be true. I'm wondering what crap I can soft-soap her with. I know I should, she's tearing up, wants me to lie, wants me to say it's going to be hunky-dory.

'Yeah … it might not last, Sam. Maybe a week, a month. You know and I know that's probably true. So why not enjoy it? Why not grab it with everything and sod what happens tomorrow?' She looks at me, and her face changes. She starts to smile, to laugh. She gives me a kiss, a hug and runs off. There's a rainbow, well … half a rainbow, and everyone's having a gawk, giving the usual *Ooh's and ah's*. I look around for Abigail and spot André coming out of the big house. I head over to him.

'I have bad news, Naseem.'

'What?'

'Your friend.'

260

Fifty-Nine

André gives me a lift. I jump out of the car, run through the hospital car park. Platform shoes not holding up too well. Nightmare. At this rate, I'll break my ankles. It's lashing down again, and there's a mental pain in my chest. I feel like screaming, bundle into reception getting fear and panic vibes from nurses. They back off, going into protection mode because I'm not making sense. My words are all stuck together. I'm banging the desk as a security guard comes running. Everything's changed to underwater ... we're all in a swimming pool, flapping about like giant turtles. How did that happen?

The guard tries to calm me down. Johnny's in the IC unit, only immediate family can see him. The head nurse is an old battle-axe. I can tell she doesn't like me. Why is that? Have you ever had that? Someone you've never met, never spoken to ... you look at them and you know they hate your guts.

'Please, for Christ's sake, I need to see my friend.' I start to lay it on, it comes easily enough. Johnny's been metal-barred. I'm not usually one for effing and blinding, but I've turned into my old man. There's a red haze in my vision, and I seem to be stepping back inside myself. I see and hear this silly kid explode and realise it's me. Another guard turns up and threatens to call the Bill. Johnny's mum hears me shouting and comes over, talks to Brunhilda, who begrudgingly says *okay* and lets me in.

I follow his mum in silence, trying to remember how to breathe. He's in this separate room with all the gear going in and out of his body. A young nurse is sat reading a book. She looks up as we enter and stands. Johnny's out of it, trundled off to darkness. His face is unrecognisable. The psychos have done a good job. I stand there, looking at him. Nothing happens. My brain is absolutely blank.

For some reason, I have this flashback to when I was a kid playing with my mate Terry. We were about six, I think, playing cowboys and Indians. Terry gets me with an arrow and I die. I liked dying. It's real somehow, special. The funny thing is, when you die, you have to fall correctly in a certain position on the ground. One of your legs has to be bent and both arms out away from your side. You couldn't die with both your legs straight out, that would be totally out of order. Also, you've got to die lying on your back. God knows why. Brunhilda comes back with a cup of tea and biscuits. Weird how your brain can be comical at such times, but then I bet Freud would've had something to say about that and all. I hate the plank.

Let me explain the Brunhilda bit. In one of his last weeks at school, before he lost it, Easton played some Wagner, *The Valkyrie*. Out of supersonic sight. I love all that Germanic stuff from reading Marvel comics. Thor was one of my favourites, but I have to say I was more drawn to Loki. He had a bit of something, a tricky gleam in his eyes. The mythical Brunhilda gets the usual from the lads, they can't get over her name, roll about calling each other Brunhilda and Siegfried. I join in as well. I know ... schoolboy humour and I'm a big boy now, but that's the way it is. It's not fair really, because apparently Brunhilda was a right goer, tough as old boots. An Amazon queen who topped herself out of heartbreak. Dear oh Lord.

Johnny's dead.

Just before it happened, I felt this calm. I noticed a fly on the wall behind his bed. It looked bored. I wondered what sort of day it had had. What do they do all day? Is time the same for them as it is for us? I could see it cleaning its legs, you know the way they do. The nurse looked up from her book and held my gaze. I think she was about to cry and went back to her book.

When his ticker stopped, the alarms went off and they herded us out of the room. I knew he'd gone. For a few minutes I knew it was alright. I knew he was laughing. His mum went berserk, hysterical, shouting at me, hitting me, blaming me for his death. I didn't say anything. Fair enough really. She blames me because I'm all he had. It must be my fault because everything's someone's fault. Maybe it is. Maybe if I'd spent more time with him. Maybe if I hadn't been with Abigail so much. Maybe ... maybe if I told his mum it's alright, that Johnny's fine, she might understand, might put her arms around me and thank me for loving him. Yeah ... maybe.

I tell André I need time alone. I walk along the prom in the rain. It's lashing it. My Timex watch says it's about midnight.

I find myself in Southdown Park, a nice little place that's out of the way, with swings and a stream. I have a go on the swings and after a while go into the play shed, have a kip.

I wake up in a tunnel, a grunting great slide that twists and tumbles, and I'm having a right laugh, bombing through at breakneck speed. Eventually it starts to narrow. I get this fear, a mammoth brick-yourself dread. I need to puke but don't seem to have a mouth, can't slow down, but I know I'm heading for something. The lights go out. All that's left is this blinding pain. It's me, my body ... I'm back in my body. Someone's talking in what sounds like a foreign language, doing something, as I'm flailing, kicking out. I don't have a clue what's going on. They hold me down, and I feel a syringe going into my backside.

Sixty

'Why didn't you come to me?' Her face is all serious. I've never seen her lovely face so serious. There are tears in her eyes, and she's sat there holding my hand. I'm hungry and my lips are all caked with dry skin. My head's an anvil that's being pummelled. Easy Easton was so narky about the use of too many similes and metaphors. I can't see what the fuss is all about. Abigail read me *The Red Pony*. Christ, I was weeping! Oh, yeah ... and not too many exclamatory interjections.

Pneumonia brought about by hypothermia and trauma. Nearly caught up with Johnny. I've been out of it for a few days apparently.

'Any chance of a snog?' I say, sort of, the words coming out strange. She leans over and kisses me on the forehead. Can't blame her for not giving me mouth-to-mouth. There's a gorgeous nurse in the background who comes over and checks my pulse and that.

'You're a very lucky young man,' she tells me.

'Here, less of the *young*. What you doing tonight?' She smiles and wanders off. Abigail's looking at me like I'm going to die at her hands. I try to laugh, but it hurts.

'What happened?' I ask.

'Some children found you. You nearly died.'

'Yeah. Weren't that bad, as it happens.' She goes over to the hospital window and looks away from me.

'Why do you do that, Naseem?' I know what she means. I try to crack jokes. I'm useless.

'I'm scared, I suppose.'

'What of … me?' She looks at me with her sweetness, concern, and I know I don't deserve her. Somehow, I feel I'm going to lose her.

'I dunno. Scared of so many things. I don't have a nice, rich dad … sorry. I don't. I don't amount. All I know is how to dance and play basketball. I love reading, but the chances of a plank like me writing anything are minimal, I'm guessing.'

'I love you, Naseem.'

There it is. The 'L' word. There's something about it that brings up the heebie-jeebies when people say it. I never believe it. It never lasts. Always turns into a prison. Anyway, I want to say it, scream it. I want to know it, mean it. Here she is. Unbelievably, she loves me. I come back to not deserving. It's not like I haven't told her. I have, loads of times, but something happens when you stop and really look at it. Most words don't have any guts, that's why I love swearing – not because it's rude, not because I can't use other words that probably make more sense. There's a connection with the magic that must once have been in all words. There's a

266

strength, a brightness that dusts the space between things. It fills it with a tingling, a warmth that bursts. The trouble with the 'L' word is it has to be backed up, has to be straight from the pit inside, the place that has no *Big Lie*. If it isn't, it starts to crumble, fade like an old black-and-white photo.

Hey, I tell you what, I read some outta sight stuff recently. This geezer called Laing and his little book called *Knots*. It was out of here, man, triple expletive. It is so true. How we talk to one another, react, double react, triple. How we defend, make things up in our heads that may or may not be happening instead of being honest, being straight with one another. No, no one does that. Well, apart from Abigail. She does me in, comes out with stuff that kills me. A few weeks ago we're having it away, there you go … we were *making love*, and she says, 'What are you thinking about?'

'What, now?'

'Yes, now.'

'Nothing.'

'Do you ever?'

'What?'

'Think, fantasise?'

'About what?'

'Other girls, women?' This girl is far out, man, she is cosmic. She says things that are so right on the button.

'I used to do that when I was on my own,' I say.

'And now?'

'No … I don't need to. I've told you how I felt at the beginning. The fear, the worry about coming.' By this time we've stopped, and I'm lying next to her.

267

'I'm worried you might get bored of me,' she says, looking up at the ceiling. See? What do you do? What do you say? I tell her I'm worried as well. 'What about?' She turns to me, leaning on her elbows.

'Christ, Abigail, what do you think? We're both so young. There's a whole world that I want to eat, taste, and I want to do it with you.'

'But?'

'Sometimes this poison starts flowing. What if we lose this? What if something goes wrong? What if you stop loving me? What if I stop ...'

'Loving me?'

'How about some toast and a cup of tea?' She gets on top of me and holds my gaze. For a while she doesn't say anything. It's so mind-blowing what she does out of the blue. I go with it. It reminds me of those games you play with mates at some point where you stare each other out. Only with Abigail there's no holding the doors, no holding anything, no fear. I go into her eyes because she's open, a river that holds your hand, pulls you in.

'I don't think fear is good, Naseem. Let's not lie to each other, even if it means we have to part.' It's as if someone else is saying it. I'm learning, but it's hard. I fall back on the old ways, ask her if she's found someone else, apologise for joking because I don't know what to say. I tell her I love her, don't want to break her heart ... but I might. She doesn't care, she's kissing my face gently, again and again, and there are tears rolling down her face. That was a few weeks ago. Johnny was still alive.

Sixty-One

Surprising how long it takes to get over the pneumonia. I've been holed up for a couple of months. Even now I'm not a hundred per cent but getting there. One good thing is knocking the fags on the head. Here, you could market that. 'Fancy giving up the cancer sticks? Have a dose of pneumonia!' I kept waiting for the bloke in the black hood and scythe to come over with a tray. 'Here's the bill, Naseem.'

Abigail and Lilly are looking after me. I'm this nineteenth-century toff convalescing in some mountain spa resort. Thomas Mann comes to mind. His writing is so crafted, a painting that has no imperfections. I remember seeing *Death in Venice* in the flicks last year, on my own. Not the sort of film the lads are into. No sex, violence or fast cars. Blew me away. There's a way of writing that sucks you into another time and place, makes you feel it's yours. It's so intimate, intelligent. I reckon it's to do with past lives. Serious. I'm getting well into the mystic, man.

Being laid up is perfect for reading. The lid came off my bonce with Carlos Castaneda's *The Teachings of Don Juan*. The

ideas in that book about other worlds, shamans, demons ...
things that can open doors to other worlds, dimensions ...
are so tempting, that after reading it I want to find a shaman.
I want to go on that adventure. I know it's probably all toss,
but who knows, maybe it's not? I'd like to think it's possible
to get to those places without drugs. There's something
about my chemistry that can't handle powerful substances
being shoved into it. There are so many roads all over the
shop – tunnels, jungles, places that are waiting to trip you
up, poison you, take you on a cosmic bash.

'Coming in?'

I'm on a lounger near the pool, and Abigail's head pops
up over the edge. She's done about seventy lengths. The
shape of her skull is perfect. With the sun glinting on her wet
face, picking out the drops, trickling down into her mouth,
sparkly chompers peeping from a half-open smile, she is
gorgeous. I look and wonder what I've done to deserve her.
I get up, take the robe off, slip gently into the warm liquid,
swim under to the far end and just about make it. Normally
I'd do two lengths, no trouble. As I come out gasping, I see
her dad has come over. He's in casual gear but always looks
sharp, a movie star in his mansion.

'Naseem, can we speak when you've got a minute? Are
you up for it?' He doesn't wait for my reply and goes back to
the house. I get out, and Abigail rubs me down with a towel.

'Get off, woman,' I say. She keeps rubbing me over
roughly. I drop the towel and look at her. She runs, I give
chase, sort of, more like a traipse. Through the vine tunnels
into the apple-tree shrubbery and on, across the tennis
courts and down the spiralling lanes to the lower depths

where the summer house waits for us at the end of a long track of flowering beds. The sanctuary of our desire. She gets naked. So do I.

'I have to see your dad,' I say, as we hold one another skin to skin in the little house. 'Your mum might walk in.' She looks at me with eyes that say, 'So what?' She's right, her mum wouldn't give a monkey's.

'Okay,' she says, breaks from me, opens the door and walks out naked. I put my shorts back on, smack her bum on the way out and trundle up to the house. When I look back at the top of the climb she's not there. Good thing really. I see how easy it is to view everything from the higher ground. After a shower I go to Samuel's office and knock on his half-open door. His voice calls me in. I enter, see he's on the phone. He motions me to sit down and speaks in French down the line, ends the conversation and looks at me.

'How are you feeling?'

'Fine,' I said. 'I'd like to thank you for letting me —'

'No need, Naseem,' he interrupts me. 'Listen, I know things have been difficult for you. What you've been through hasn't been easy,' he says. I can see he's being genuine, but I don't want a *father/son* chat.

'I'd rather not talk about it, Samuel.'

'I understand.' He gets up, goes to the patio doors and looks out. 'I was wondering, Naseem, now that you're getting better, if you've given any thought to my offer of work?' He sits back down and waits. I wait.

'The thing is, Samuel, please don't take this wrong, but I'd like to be like you. I want to be my own boss. I don't want any favours, short cuts. I want to get there under my own

271

steam.' He smiles, and I see where Abigail gets hers from. It's a nice smile, not snide.

'That's good to hear, Naseem, and I take no offence. On the contrary, it shows you've got something. Have you any idea what it is you'd like to do?'

'I want to be a writer. I'll see if I can get my job back at the restaurant. I'd like to contribute something, Samuel. It probably won't be much, but it would make me feel better.'

'We'll talk about that later,' he says. 'In the meantime, take as long as you need and don't rush into getting back to work.' That was it. I was about to go when I opened my mouth. I have a tendency to do that now and then.

'Samuel, can I ask you something?'

'Of course.'

'I don't know where to start. The thing is ... you've allowed me into your home, looked after me, I live with your daughter, we're both kids ... yet you seem fine about it. I know we've spoken about this before, her health and all that, but it still doesn't make sense.'

'It is strange, isn't it?' He went over to where a coffee maker was percolating and poured out a cup. 'Coffee?'

'No, I'm fine, thanks.'

'Let me ask you something. How's your relationship with your parents?' Out of the blue. Taras would love this bloke's money and prestige, he'd be trying to suck up and make friends. Maybe I'll introduce him. Belly laugh.

'Never got on with my old man, love my mum.' Keep it plain and simple.

'Say you wanted to stay out when you were fourteen, what would your father say? Suppose he said, "Fine, no problem.

272

Here's some money. Go on, have some fun," what would you think?'

'I'd think he's having a laugh or it's some trap.'

'How do you think Abigail would feel if I denied her the right to see you? How would she feel about me?'

'What if she wanted to take drugs? What if I was a right waster who was out to use her?'

He drinks some of his coffee. 'I'm a good judge of character, Naseem, and when the time is right she may try everything and see she doesn't need them.' He is quiet for a while, but the chat isn't over. 'I'm not an advocate for the *anything goes* way of life, but neither do I believe in rules that are unjust, ignorant. How did you learn about basketball? Did you read about it? Did you listen to what someone else told you and copy it?' I can see what he is saying. Learning has to be something you want to do otherwise it's all tosh, meaningless.

'Suppose it all goes wrong?' I ask.

'How?' I can tell he is enjoying all this. I have to admit, so was I. It's rare to find someone so up front. 'If you and Abigail break up, is that what you mean? Who knows? Maybe you won't. Maybe she'll die of her condition.' There is no menace there, nothing clever. He is saying it as it is, straight up. It still knocks me for six. 'Naseem, as long as Abigail is enjoying her life, that's all I care about. Perhaps you feel I'm using you.' He pauses, is silent for a while. 'I am using you, Naseem. Everyone uses everyone else, even if they love them; they do so out of a selfish sense of possession. Now listen, I'm not here to prove anything. The thing is, I'd like us to be honest with each other. You're one of the family. The only rule is honesty.'

273

That is the end of the chat. I walk out not sure what I'm supposed to feel. The guy's a maniac, but I love maniacs. I head up to Abigail who's doing some homework. She looks up at me.

'You okay?'

'Yeah. Your dad's the boss.'

Sixty-Two

Easton's making dinner. I watch as he dices vegetables and chunters about the Greeks and how everything follows a mythic structure. It's a bit over my head, if I'm honest, but basically, stories have similar bits that follow one another. I think it's his way of talking about Johnny without talking about him. I've told him what happened. I don't think Johnny would mind. In fact, I asked him, and he said, *Yeah, Naz, man. Keep the flame not the smoke, brother.* Funny that. It's not something he's ever said before. Yeah, I speak to him. Out loud when I'm alone and quietly, in my bonce, when I'm with people. He always answers. Of course, it could just be me.

Johnny and Penny never made it to the annexe. In the last few weeks he started slapping her about. Her dad found out. That was the end of the truce. Charlie's boys weren't meant to kill Johnny. It was supposed to be a warning, but he was so drunk, he kept getting up, trying to lay into them. He did more harm to himself falling about. I learnt all this from Penny last week. She rang me, sobbing uncontrollably. She

275

loved him, I know, but Johnny was lost. He couldn't cope with it all. His worst nightmare had come true. He was trapped. He wasn't in love. He was lonely.

'*It is the stars. The stars above us govern our conditions. Else one self mate and mate could not beget such different issues.*' Easton loves The Bard. Quotes him as he puts potatoes he's cut up in the oven with oil, rosemary, garlic, butter, salt and pepper. Knows his onions, the lazy tyke.

'How often do you cook, Harry?'

'I prefer *Easy,* please, Naseem. It reminds me of the lemmings I've left behind to the winds of oblivion. In answer to your impertinent question, it's a love thing. Samantha, my glorious beloved, and I take it in turns as the spirit moves us.' He cleans up, and we go into the lounge where the log fire's dancing, crackling with fun. Samantha's reading *Watership Down.* She's barefoot, in pyjamas and silk dressing gown with dragons and tigers. The room's vibing friendly, but I know by now that nothing's what it seems.

'Any good?'

'It is, Naseem. Surprisingly so.'

'*Good.* I suppose Enid Blyton's worthy of that epithet?' Easy's wit can still be slicing, but it seems to have lost its nastiness. They both look like they've got through something. Come out the other side. 'Naseem, I've spoken to Jemima recently. I've taken the liberty of sending her your love story. She'd like to enter it in a competition, with your permission. Well, what do you think?'

I stayed till about four and left them arguing about rabbits and the merits of anthropomorphism. Yeah, I can write and pronounce all sorts of ponce these days. I catch a bus to Taras

Bulba mansions, bought with grandad's corrupt money. Mum opens the door and gives me a hug. She'd been round several times to see me, but I'd been out of it. She and the Dambois family are as thick as thieves, it seems. She really hit it off with Lilly.

'Naseem, he's not in the best of moods.' I laugh. After a bit she does as well, and I tell her I don't care, I want to see Jamal and Iman. She shows me around the big house they've bought with grandad's dosh, all the nice deco and furniture. It's a real home. Taras is picking his nose and watching telly. He pretends I'm not there. It's quite late by now, and the kids are in their room, which is done up bright, full of normal stuff, toys, colourful wallpaper. I'm a bit taken back. Jamal and Iman give me a hug. We play games for half an hour, have a laugh. Mum asks the usual. I tell her I'm fine and going back to work soon.

I say goodbye, am about to go when something makes me do something mental. I go over to the old man and speak to him, ask him if I can have a word. He looks at me suspiciously. He's as puzzled as I am and not sure how to respond.

'What?' he says after a pause full of blood-drenched knives. What I say next is a bit out of focus, a little bit insane. It doesn't make sense yet makes complete sense. I don't recognise myself as I'm saying it. I think I might be in some parallel dimension that's about to collapse. It doesn't. The words have all gone. I can't remember. The spluttering, pauses, the shaking of my body. I tell him I love him, want us to be friends or at least try and get on without hating one another. I tell him I'm sorry for the agro I've caused, thank

277

him for looking after me. I don't know what else I said, but there was a sort of yellow light in my vision, a blurring that came with a distant whine, ever so cold, far away. I heard myself saying stuff as if I was somewhere else, some insect up on the ceiling. There I was, opening and closing my mouth. Mum's gob's open as well, and she's gone into a trance. I'm about to leave when he gets up.

'Naseem.' He hasn't called me by my name for years. I turn around expecting him to start. He tries to say something, tries to say something, tries to say …. but he can't. In that instant I can see his whole life collapse in his body. He sits down in his chair with a thud, gives an automatic outbreath of air, the sort that comes before you sob. He doesn't, though. Well, that is it. I go over and … we hug – for one second. One second before his body goes rigid. We have done all we could. It is massive. At the steps to the outside door mum starts bawling to finish things off. I hug her, tell her I love her. She seems so frail, like a sparrow. Most of the time we walk about with this aura of who we are, and once in a blue moon it vanishes and there's the real. It's so vulnerable we can't bear it, shrug it off, hide it.

It's the dog's bollocks.

Sixty-Three

Abigail's changed her mind. She's taking her A levels and going to university. That's the plan. I have to say, I'm quite pleased. London would be great but not yet. A couple of years maybe. I ask what made her change her mind.

'I don't want to be away from you any more than I have to, Naseem. Acting can wait. In a couple of years I might try to get into one of the main drama schools. I had this idea.'

The female of the species, as Kipling was fond of saying, *is deadlier than the male.* I think he meant women are far more intelligent than us blokes, and I'm there, man, one hundred per cent. Abigail pushes the idea of night school into my head – how I could retake some GCEs with her help and maybe, who knows, even an English A level. I mull it over while we're cuddling in bed, say I'll think about it. It does ring an appealing bell somewhere, as it happens. I want to learn about writing so much. Easy Easton is magic, but somehow I get the feeling I can't depend on him. Abigail's taking music and drama in sixth form, wants me to start going to the drama group. Yeah, man, I'm in there like a snake being charmed. I'm walking on those hot coals with the shamans. Brothers and sisters, the moon is in the seventh house. A supersonic, galactic happening.

We had the chat with Lilly. She didn't mess around. I thought it was going to be something like *The Joy of Sex*, you know, mutual pleasuring, satisfying one another. Techniques to please your partner. How to do this and that. All that stuff makes me laugh. That's why I was a bit on edge. No, man. It blew me away. She opens her mouth and all this magic comes out. Liquid gold. Making love is sacred, an ancient ceremony people have forgotten. It's a pathway to the stars, big medicine. Nothing to do with humping and bumping. I'm there, wide-eyed and drinking it up. Thing is, it's a whole mind-and-heart thing that means changing it all. Starting from scratch. I'm in, brother, but shaking with it.

Sixty-Four

One morning I wake up early. Abigail's deep in slumber. I quietly get dressed in my best togs, pick up my cassette player and head off towards the station. I get a bus to Portslade and on the way to the cemetery buy some flowers from a corner shop. By the time I get there I'm glad I brought my camel coat. It's a bleak September morning with red smears across the distant horizon over the sea. Underneath the coat I'm wearing the trousers Johnny borrowed, the light-blue flares, his white tear-drop shirt, fake-gold necklace and black platforms.

The cemetery's empty, as they usually are. That's the good thing about them really, best places to go if you want to be quiet. I found Johnny's grave straight off. Even after two months, there's a freshness about newcomers. Next to him is a rickety wooden bench where I sit down, have a gander.

I love the change in the seasons, especially autumn. The light seems softer, the smells stronger, what's the word … pungent. They hit you, bowl you over in a way you've forgotten they can. And the little midges, the insects, have nearly all gone, and those that are left seem drunk, slow and dozy. They come out and dance with a sort of arrogance that says, *We're still here. We're survivors, mate.* I do miss my favourite summer friends, the swifts. They've legged it back to Africa. I won't see them for another year. The nutters can be a menace in town, howling and screeching at head height. If I could be an animal, that's what I'd be, I reckon. They seem to have such a laugh and the way they fly is mental. Mind you, I don't suppose the midges are too enamoured. Enamoured? Easton must be about.

If you're lucky there comes a stillness in autumn that opens a door. Blink your eyes in the right way, and King Arthur might pop around the corner on his horse. I swear I sometimes see fairies, but the little blighters are too quick, they scarper when you look closer. That's the trouble these days, we seem to have lost the magic.

Talking of magic, one day me and Johnny were kicking a football outside his house. Johnny's amazing with the skills, he could bounce forever. He starts heading it, counting, and this car comes along the narrow road, wants to go by.

'Oy, Johnny, get over here,' I shout, but he takes no notice. The geezers in the car come out and he keeps going. A crowd of kids start gathering, by this time there are other cars, people looking out their windows. He's reached two hundred, and everyone's counting. There are about fifty people watching, shouting, and Johnny's mum comes out.

'Johnny! Get inside.' He takes no notice. Gets to three hundred, finally heads it high up into the crowd. Crowds are a bit mad. There's an energy comes over them that's a bit insane, herd-like. That's what Huxley was talking about in one of his essays. Oh yes, Aldous (I love you) Huxley. He is my God. Well, one of them. The crowd goes wild, grabs Johnny, lifts him on their shoulders. They're all chanting 'Johnny! Johnny!' Some granny must have got on the blower because the Bill skid up with their sirens; they don't half love all that. I blame Steve McGarrett of *Hawaii Five-O*.

I'm getting a stiff bum from sitting on the bench. I've been here three hours. There are too many clichés about time passing, time stopping, turning back on itself. If Einstein's right and it's all a circle where we go back or start all over again, what a nightmare. I get up, stretch, place the cassette player on my friend's grave, press play. It blares out Marvin's liquid soul. He's singing 'What's Going On'. It starts out at a friendly party. Check it out. The people are getting down with the love and peace, man. Sure, they're of the streets, but they love the earth, love the planet. They join with the freshness of friends back from Vietnam that know the pain, know the joy. He tells it straight from the heart, to me and you, to a child. A lullaby of pleading that asks why we do what we do. It's all there, man. The injustice, unemployment, needless cruelty. Why do we do it? What's going on?

I start dancing, slow and smoochy, and the whole cemetery starts to dance with me. After a while they're all here: the old fellers, old dears, all the kids that went early, all the mums, dads, aunties, going back to God knows when. We have a right laugh. Johnny's not here. Maybe he'll turn up in a bit. I bet he's combing his locks in some angelic hairdressers. I ask this old geezer in Victorian garb if he knows where he is?

283

'Did you never hear of a place that goes by the name of *Limbo*?' he asks with an Irish accent that's high pitched, sing-songy. He stares at me with the twinkle, daring me to ask the next question.

'What's he doing there?'

'Sure, you little eejit, do ya not know a thing at all about the hereafter? Well, I won't spoil it for you, Nazzy. You'll find out soon enough.' With that he winks at me and toddles off. A little girl in a summer dress, holding a parasol, comes over and smiles.

'Johnny's being transformed.'

'Into what?'

'Love. Your memory of him will fade in a while. It takes time. You can't remember love. It's always here. It's not memorable.'

'What do you mean *Your memory of him*?'

'The real part of Johnny never dies,' she said. 'The shadows will fade but his essence will always be with you.' There's a buzzing sound near my ear. I instinctively swat away a huge bumblebee. By the time I look again the party's over. Everyone's gone. All I can see are rows and rows of graves with flowers and crosses. The wind picks up, and it starts to rain. There's a band of pain across my chest and I'm shaking, trembling, finding it hard to breathe. Thankfully Marvin comes raging back into my blood with 'Inner City Blues'. I throw off my coat, and I'm up, giving it welly. And I dance, man. I dance like I've never danced in my life and never will again. I dance with my mate and we are on fire. We are *The Funk Brothers*. We are the magic. The groove explodes, burns with the changing light, the pounding rain. Burns with all the things that have to die for life to come again. This groove ... this thing inside ... what is it? I don't know. Don't want to know.

I leave the cassette playing and leg it.

Johnny never spoke to me again.